If he wanted to, the man could just lift that gun up a bit, and shoot her now.

He could shoot Nate, he could shoot everyone on this carriage. This train.

Fear tightened her throat, settled heavy on her chest.

It would be *so* easy to lean into it, to lean into the fear and let it overwhelm her. But she didn't allow it, she couldn't.

Rather than leaning into the fear, Lou leaned back into Nate's chest, and his arm around her grew tighter. She could feel his heartbeat, its rhythm steady and strong. He was warm, *hot* really, against the thin cotton of her singlet, and in pretty much any other situation being so completely pressed against his body – back, hips, butt – would've been ... something else. Intimate. Sexy.

But right now, of course it wasn't. It wasn't about Nate being a man and her being a woman, or about their history, as ancient as it was.

It was his strength and hers.

Together.

FOR THE FIGHT

ELITE SWAT BOOK ONE

LEAH ASHTON

ISBN 978-0-6484400-6-2

First edition published November 2018 (as *Undaunted*)

This second edition first published March 2020 (as *For the Fight*)

For Eve, who is awesome
(and who I might let read this one day)

CHAPTER ONE

Today, Luella Brayshaw was planting a bomb.

On this perfect, cloudless Perth morning, while the Swan River sparkled and the sun beat down on the hundreds of tourists that meandered around Elizabeth Quay.

Admittedly it was only a fake bomb – or rather – the *concept* of a bomb. This was a training exercise, after all, and the backpack she carried contained no more than the clothes she'd so painstakingly chosen for her first day at Elite SWAT Headquarters – only to discover she would *not* simply be answering phones today.

But still. It felt like far too nice a day to even be *thinking* about blowing anything up. After twelve years in the police force, Lou should know more than most that awful things happened despite a postcard-worthy backdrop. In real life, bad guys certainly didn't need murky camera angles or a foreboding soundtrack. Shitheads just did shithead things.

And sometimes during those shithead things, experienced police officers make stupid mistakes.

And ended up on desk duties at Elite SWAT – or rather, *not* on desk duties, but instead walking around aimlessly at Elizabeth Quay, pretending they had a bomb in their backpack.

Honestly, it would be difficult for this situation to be any more humiliating.

Her entire career, Lou's colleagues and sergeants had encouraged her to consider a move to the Elite SWAT team. A constable with her talent and track record would surely aspire to work with the best of the best, right? Elite SWAT – or E-SWAT - had everything: a tactical response team, dignitary protection, covert surveillance, bomb technicians, negotiators, snipers – every specialist team in the police had been brought together under the Elite SWAT umbrella.

But Lou had never been interested. It had *always* been grassroots policing that had been her passion: being a part of the community she protected and served. She wanted to help with everyday problems that rarely got the attention they needed, and certainly never ended up in the news: like the young woman who'd finally felt safe enough to press charges against her abusive partner, or the elderly residents being scammed by unscrupulous door-to-door salesmen. No one wrote a front-page article when she let an impressionable first-time twelve-year-old shoplifter off with a warning – and a tour of the lock-up and a sombre lecture of *exactly* how their life would pan out if they continued to make such stupid, selfish decisions.

By contrast, barely a week went by without the WA media lauding some huge E-SWAT-led success story. There were, of course, countless other success stories that never made it public.

But that didn't appeal to Lou. You needed great cops to deal with the big stuff that Elite SWAT dealt with daily. But you also needed great cops to deal with the small stuff left to everyone else.

Except – now no one thought Lou was a great cop.

One day, one mistake, and she was reduced to *this*.

A fill-in for an actress who'd called in sick. Wearing one of the female Elite SWAT operator's spare clothes: jeans that were just a bit too big, a white tank top that was just a bit too small.

But it would have to do. The one day she'd ever rocked up to work in heels, a pencil skirt, and blouse (hey, if she was going to be relegated to desk duties she was going to look good doing it), she'd had to get changed out of her beautiful new clothes almost immediately.

Thankfully she'd had a pair of sneakers in her car she could wear – dark blue suede with pink stripes – so yeah, fashionable rather than practical, but certainly better than walking through Perth in her heels or a stranger's work boots. And she had a lot of walking to do today.

Just act natural, her sergeant had said, after he'd

dropped her off beneath the glinting glass and copper of the Bell Tower. *Wait for my call.*

Acting natural had taken her for a walk from the Bell Tower and Barrack Street Jetty, and across to the small man-made island that jutted out at the mouth of the quay. Children laughed and shrieked as they swarmed a wooden tower-dotted playground, and the small kiosk at the island's centre tempted her with the allure of caffeine – but she had no idea if purchasing a takeaway latte was allowed. Do fake bombers carry coffee cups?

Old Lou would've asked her new sergeant all about the exercise in the short drive in from Elite SWAT headquarters to the city. But this new version of Lou had felt the weight of derision and reluctant obligation emanating from Sergeant Peters. Lou had no idea why or how she'd been dumped at Elite SWAT, but clearly Peters wasn't a fan.

So, she'd sat silently like the gutless loser everyone now thought she was, and now had no idea what was going to happen today, or what she was actually allowed to do, other than wait for Peters' phone call. After that, she'd make her way to an unknown destination, covertly followed by who knew how many E-SWAT operators.

As she left the island via the swooping, dramatic curves of the pedestrian bridge that traversed the gently rippling Swan River, her skin prickled with awareness. Were eyes on her now? They must be, the operators on this exercise couldn't have been too far away.

Self-consciously, she tugged at the too short hem of

her tank top as she passed yet another couple taking selfies on the bridge, Perth's collection of glass and metal sky scrapers rising above the quay behind them.

Her phone rang just after she stepped off the bridge and onto the western promenade, and Lou tugged it out of the back pocket of her borrowed Levis.

Peters didn't bother with *hello*. "Perth Train Station. Don't walk straight there, act like someone who doesn't want to be followed. Reckon you can do that?"

His lack of faith in her was palpable.

"Of course."

Peters grunted. "Pay attention to anyone you notice following you. If you do, try to lose 'em. Got it?"

"Got it," Lou said, but he'd already hung up. "Arse-hole," she added, to the black screen of the phone before shoving it back into her pocket.

Then, she took a deep breath, tucked the escaped strands of long brown hair she'd so carefully braided this morning behind her ears, and straightened her shoulders.

She'd do anything to change what had happened two weeks ago, to change the decision that had landed her here. But she couldn't.

She had mandated counselling and training to complete before she got her firearm back and life went back to normal. She might not like it – and based on Peters' reaction, Elite SWAT might not like it either – but for now, she was stuck with them.

And so, because Luella Brayshaw never did anything

half way, she was going to be the best damn fake bomber they'd ever seen.

NATE RIVERS HELD his long-empty takeaway coffee cup to his lips as he waited for the target to exit the arcade behind him.

He kept his gaze on the window display directly in front of him, the glass providing a clear view of the narrow arcade in its reflection. To a casual onlooker – or to a target being followed – he looked like a typical suit in between meetings.

Although, he hadn't quite stretched to wearing the jacket part of the navy-blue suit he kept back at Elite SWAT headquarters for CBD-related surveillance. It was just too hot in Perth in March to wear a jacket. Nate figured that in this scenario, he just worked somewhere with a fairly relaxed dress code. And in that spirit, he'd also tossed his tie and popped open the top few buttons of his shirt – although not so many as to expose the narrow, paper-thin band of the microphone collar beneath the crisp white fabric.

"Target about to enter Murray Street Mall, heading west. White singlet, pink stripes on shoes, dark hair in plait." The voice in his hidden earpiece was clear and succinct.

"Got her," Nate said, as the woman stepped from the darkness of the arcade into the bright sunlight of the pedestrian mall.

"All yours, mate."

Nate waited a beat before turning, watching the woman pause and retrieve her phone from the back pocket of her jeans. But she wasn't really looking at the phone. As he watched, she subtly glanced up and down the mall and then over her shoulder. Her gaze didn't even skim over Nate; there were at least twenty people between him and the woman at any moment in time. The wave of shoppers, tourists, and workers was constant and effectively camouflaged him from view.

He couldn't see her all that clearly in the window's reflection either. About all he knew was that the woman was about average height, slender without being skinny, and her hair was in a thick, brunette braid.

Apparently satisfied with her survey of the mall, the woman turned left, towards Forest Chase, stepping into the wake of a large group of teenage girls. As Nate watched, she moved through the group, and then he lost her as they walked between a café and its alfresco seating and market umbrellas, his view obscured.

A moment later, when the girls continued down the mall, the woman wasn't there.

This was new. As he'd listened to the target's progress along the kilometre journey from the quay to Perth train station – only a few hundred metres beyond where he stood – she'd taken twists and turns – doubling back on herself, alternatively ducking into shadows and walking in plain sight, and even travelling a short distance on one of the city's zero-fare buses that constantly looped through the CBD. She'd almost lost her tail then, but knowing the fixed route of the bus the team had deployed operators to all upcoming stops and picked her up again as she'd alighted. But still – if this exercise had involved a smaller team, the manoeuvre might have worked.

Of course, the guy on her arse should've worked out what she was doing *before* she'd got on the bus – but then, that was the point of this exercise. The team today was made up of tactical operators, including himself. They didn't normally do a lot of surveillance, they were more about taking targets down once all this work had been done: like waking up pieces of shit at three in the morning with red dots on their foreheads for arrest warrants, stopping some gun-toting arsehole from shooting people, or intercepting million-dollar meth hauls.

But like all the operators at Elite SWAT, they needed to have a working knowledge of everything Elite SWAT did. He might not be a bomb tech or a negotiator or whatever, but he knew a hell of a lot more than the average beat cop, and he needed to, never knowing what the next job would bring.

So, yeah, he wasn't about to lose this target.

Nate crossed the mall to drop his coffee cup into a bin located near the café. The woman only had two options – she was either in the café, or the adjacent accessories shop. All they needed to do was cover the exits – each had only a single door in and out, which he had covered – and he spoke quietly into his microphone to direct the nearest operators to cover any exit out the rear.

Then, he simply walked straight past both shops and took a seat on a bench in the centre of the mall, facing away. Then watched the opposite shop windows to see what happened next.

Minutes later, she reappeared.

This time, she didn't pause. She was out the door of the accessories shop, then off, walking briskly towards Forest Chase.

Nate hesitated before following her. Partly because he couldn't be that obvious, but mostly because something about her walk triggered something … *reminded* him of something. Of someone.

The way the woman walked – the neat posture, the determined strides, even the swing of her arms – he *knew* that walk.

But that was impossible.

Actors were always used for these exercises, and the woman she reminded him of, was – last time he checked – still a cop.

Not that he kept tabs on her, or anything. Just occasionally, he wondered how she was doing after all this time. Curiosity, nothing more.

Nate stood, and began to follow the woman down the mall.

Lou HAD to admit that the E-SWAT guys were *good*.

Despite *knowing* she was being followed every step of her walk from the quay to the train station there'd been only one time she'd been pretty sure she'd spotted an operator. A guy in board shorts, singlet and thongs – his outfit in itself nondescript, his ripped deltoids and biceps not so much. Even then she'd been unsure, he certainly hadn't been obviously following her. It was more a *feeling*. Yet when she'd jumped on that bus, she was almost certain she'd seen what could only be described as an *Oh Fuck* expression on his face as the bus zipped away.

She had to admit, it'd been rather satisfying.

Now, as she crossed the overpass between Forrest Chase and the double-storey train station, she wasn't entirely sure what to do. Was the exercise over the moment she stepped into the building?

As she did exactly that – a bakery to her right, and the station information and ticket stand to her left – nothing happened.

Lou grinned. What had she expected?

She came to a stop just in front of the ticket gates, then turned around, imagining the final operator who'd been tailing her would be behind her and could tell her where to go next. Or maybe Sergeant Peters would call her, as surely, he'd be well aware she'd reached her destination.

Or maybe she should call him? She reached for her phone, only to go absolutely still as she recognised a man not even ten metres away from her.

A tall man with dark, army-short hair and dark blue eyes. A man with broad shoulders and tanned skin revealed from wrist to elbow by the shoved-up sleeves of his snowy-white shirt.

The planes of his face were different – *harder*, which made sense. It'd been more than ten years. Nate Rivers had gone from young man, to man. He'd been gorgeous back then, but now, 100 percent grown up? He was devastating.

Nate's gaze met hers.

She watched as his eyes widened, and as his gaze swept up and down her body. Was he cataloguing her changes, too?

Longer hair, better make-up, a few extra kilos from when she was twenty-one. How did she stack up?

Why did she care?

She didn't. She didn't care *at all* what Nate Rivers thought of her.

What was she doing? Nothing had changed. They had nothing to say to each other.

Without thinking, she turned away. She needed to move, to get away from him.

Stupid, unwanted prickles tightened her throat, stung her eyes.

Hell no. She was *not* going to let Nate see her tears.

That horrifying possibility propelled her forward, into the crowd of commuters.

Why would she waste tears on him? Where had they

even come from? She was over him. She had to be – it had been forever.

A lifetime ago.

She realised she was at the ticket gates. With no ticket, of course. Around her, card readers beeped merrily, while she held up the line. *What to do?*

"Luella?"

No.

Even his voice sounded older. Richer.

And too close to her, definitely too close to her.

Beside her, a mother was waved through a wider gate with a pram, and Lou simply stepped in behind her.

The transit guard either didn't notice or didn't care, and grateful, she almost ran to the escalator that would take her down to the platforms below.

She didn't look back as she jogged down the moving steps, springing onto the platform without looking back, her gaze darting about. Where to go now?

"*Lou*," Nate said, even closer now, but she wouldn't turn around. "Wait, please."

A train sat, doors open, at the platform. Before she could think, she was on the train. Surely, he wouldn't follow her onto it?

She collapsed onto one of the chairs near the front of the carriage, one that backed against the wall and faced another line of empty seats before her.

Lou had gone to great pains to know nothing of what Nate was doing now. She'd never Facebook stalked him, never Googled him.

Given his clothing, he'd clearly left the police – she never would've expected that. He had a whole new life she knew nothing about, cared nothing about.

Liar.

Suddenly – far too belatedly – the idiocy of what she was doing crashed down on her.

Sergeant Peters would surely call her any moment. Or an Elite SWAT operator was about to ask her what the hell she was doing.

She needed to get off this train and pull herself together.

She rushed to her feet, but it was too late.

The doors closed before her, and immediately her gaze went to the network map printed on the carriage wall. She'd just get off at the next stop.

No problem. She'd sort this out.

"Lou," Nate said, right beside her. "What the hell are you doing?"

And that was when what should've been blindingly obvious hit her.

Hit her, just as she forced herself to meet his gaze.

Nate had not quit the force to work in an office.

He was not following her because he desperately needed to talk to her or see her again, or something equally unlikely and fantastical.

No. He was an E-SWAT operator.

It was his job to follow her.

That was all.

"Fuck," she said.

CHAPTER TWO

Fuck.

The word hung between them as the train pulled away from the station.

Lou held Nate's gaze *hard*, as if she was proving a point.

But Nate couldn't read her expression. She was pissed, sure. But at him? Herself? The situation?

"I didn't know you were the target," he said. "Not until we reached the train station."

Not for sure, at least. He'd been 99 percent sure as he'd watched her dart through the perfume counters at Myer, not quite close enough to be certain, but close enough to know he knew the sway of those hips. The set of that jaw. It was only the incongruity of Lou playing the target that didn't fit.

Lou shrugged. "I didn't know you worked at Elite

SWAT," she said. "Otherwise I wouldn't have …" Her gaze darted briefly out the window.

"Run away?" he prompted.

That hard gaze was back. "I …"

He knew she was about to deny it, but then he watched her reconsider. This was typical Lou, as honest as they came.

"I didn't want to talk to some dick who treated me like shit a decade ago," she said. "What was I supposed to do?"

Nate blinked. That was more honest that he was expecting. *Bolder* than he'd expected. Lou had always been strong, but also always a little shy. A bit reserved.

With maturity had come confidence. *Good for her.*

The carriage jostled as the train took a curve, and she grabbed for one of the hand straps hanging from the roof to regain her balance.

The action revealed several inches of olive skin as her tank top slid upwards.

Nate made himself look away, knowing she was right about him being a dick a decade ago and not wanting to be one again now. They were work colleagues it seemed. He had to be professional.

Lou tugged at her top with her spare hand, and he saw the hint of a blush on her cheeks.

Damn. He *knew* that blush. A memory hit him hard and crystal clear: Lou on his bed, on her knees, the T-shirt she'd just tugged off for him bunched in her hands in front of her body. *That* blush, and then her gaze had met his and whatever she'd seen had been enough to make her drop the shirt, and reach for him without hesitation. Beautiful, and brave, and sexy as hell.

Beautiful.

Professionalism be damned, he couldn't stop himself from looking at her for long moments, as the train swayed and rattled its way to the next station. She looked different, of course – her hair was longer, and it didn't have the blonde streaks she'd used to get done. But her blue-green eyes were just the same: big and intense; and her nose slender and jaw sharp.

He'd thought her hot the first time he'd seen her as a cadet. He'd realised she was smart and stubborn – and just as determined as him shortly after.

He met her gaze which was still hard, her eyes narrowed.

"Why were you the target today?" he asked, as if he wasn't thinking about how her hips had used to feel under his hands. How his thumb had fitted against the jut of her hip bones, and how his fingers would flare out and grip her heated skin as they …

"I'm working at Elite SWAT for a bit," she said, her tone prickly. He reckoned she knew exactly what he was thinking about. "Desk duties," she added, "it's temporary."

Those words did snap him out of the past.

"Why?" he asked, stunned. Why on earth would a

cop like Lou be off the street? Desk duties were for when something went wrong: a mistake, an investigation, an injury. "Are you okay?"

"Of course," she said. "And I'm sure you'll hear the gossip about why I'm at E-SWAT soon enough. I won't spoil it for you."

Her gaze did *not* invite him pushing the point. Besides she was right. E-SWAT was not a place to keep a secret. Top-secret operations involving months of planning and not a whisper mentioned to a soul outside those involved? No problem. The place was a fucking vault. But anything personal? Scandalous? Or even just mildly, vaguely embarrassing? You might as well just send out a group email and not even bother hoping to keep it on the down-low.

But Nate did *not* like the idea of the team talking about Lou. He *knew* her. If something had gone wrong, it hadn't been her fault. He hated the idea that the other operators would judge her. Would dismiss her.

He saw it all the time. You needed an ego to be at E-SWAT, that went without saying. The men and women were used to being the best, the most talented – and when they got to E-SWAT they were surrounded by more of the best, more of the most talented. It was competitive, and it was intense.

And there was a hierarchy. It was bloody difficult to get through the E-SWAT selection course, to get your foot in the door. When you did, you were – as the team name made clear - marked as *elite*. Better than the rest, and superior to every other cop in the state.

But Nate knew it wasn't that simple. He'd always wanted to be a cop, and was always going follow in his father's footsteps. But his dad hadn't been part of Elite SWAT. He'd 'just' been a sergeant in a regional town.

But he'd been Nate's hero. And simply by being a great cop, he'd been a shit tonne of other people's hero too.

Being a great cop, like he knew Lou was, mattered. If you were at E-SWAT or not.

"I'll set them straight," he said. "Don't worry about it."

The train was slowing as it arrived at City West station. They'd need to get off here and catch the next train back.

"You will *not* do that," Lou said, dropping the hand strap so she could step closer to him. They'd already been standing relatively close, but now she was near enough that she needed to tilt her chin to meet his gaze. "Don't you *dare*. I can look after myself. Besides, Nate, I *did* fuck up, all right? So, nothing to set straight. Probably whatever gossip you hear will be true."

The train rolled to a complete stop. A young woman with a baby asleep in one of those baby sling things stood at the door, ready to alight. Outside, only a few people dotted the station platform. It was late morning on a Monday – not exactly peak hour for the Perth to Fremantle line.

"No way," Nate said, as the doors slid open. "That doesn't sound like the Lou I knew. Tell me what happened, there's got to be more to it—"

"There's not, Nate," she said on a sigh. "Come on, let's just get off this stupid train."

Nate activated his microphone as he waited for the mother and baby to step off in front of him. He'd already let the team know he'd followed the target onto the platform and then onto the train.

He'd completely ignored Peters' ranting about Lou not understanding simple instructions, and besides – Peters had calmed down pretty quick. It wasn't much more than three minutes from Perth to City West. They'd added maybe ten minutes to the exercise, and they'd all be back at headquarters for the debrief before they knew it.

"At City West with the target. We'll catch the—"

Lou's hand on his arm instantly silenced him.

Initially it was just because she'd touched him – even through the thin cotton fabric of his shirt the simple act of her hand on him instantly focused all of his attention.

But swiftly, it stopped being about a visceral, primal reaction to Lou as a woman, and became completely about what she was trying to tell him.

She'd curled her hand just above his elbow, her fingers digging into his bicep.

"*Wait*," she said, urgently, under her breath.

As the woman and her baby stepped out of the train

and onto the platform, a man and another woman hurried through the carriage door.

Well, more accurately – the man hurried. The man was only of average height, but he was constructed of inflated muscle, with huge shoulders and pectorals beneath the snug black T-shirt he wore. His muscular arms were liberally covered in tattoos, with the artwork presumably continuing under the fabric of his shirt, reappearing above his collar to wrap around his neck.

Rather than take one of the many spare seats in the nearly empty carriage, the guy dragged the woman to a stop immediately across from the still open carriage door.

His dark hair was short, his features blunt. His jaw was clenched.

Now, Nate had nothing against tattoos. Tatts could be cool. Not his thing personally, but heaps of the guys at E-SWAT had them. Likewise, he got the whole gym thing. He was paid to be fit. Extremely fit.

So, having tatts and being ripped didn't make you a bad guy.

But Nate had been in the job long enough to know a shithead when he saw one. And this guy, with his arm wrapped around the waist of the woman beside him, was pure shithead.

Whether his criminality extended beyond intimidating women, Nate had no idea. But he had absolutely no doubt the small woman standing beside the man did *not* want to be on this train.

He glanced at Lou.

But she'd already stepped around him, crossing the carriage to stand before the woman. The woman hadn't looked up the entire time Nate had been watching, her blonde hair covering her face in a tangled curtain.

"Are you okay?" Lou asked her, as Nate stepped up beside her.

The shithead was entirely focused on Lou, his anger almost a tangible thing – like an aura of fury surrounding him. He was older than Nate had thought, probably late forties, with salt and pepper through his almost buzz cut hair. He held the blonde woman tight, her body pressed against his from shoulder to hip. The muscles in the arm wrapped around her were tensed, and veins popped on the back of his hand and up his arms. A similar vein pulsed on the man's forehead as he glared at Luella.

A beeping noise heralded the closing of the carriage doors behind Nate.

It seemed they weren't going to get back to Elite SWAT headquarters as quickly as he'd thought. But that was okay. You don't just look the other way – ever.

Lou would've asked the woman if she was okay whether she was in uniform or not. So would he.

But – the thing was they *weren't* in uniform, and the shithead had no idea that two police officers stood in front of him. *Unarmed* police officers, given neither of them had needed a firearm for the surveillance exercise, and gun legislation in Australia didn't allow even the police to conceal carry without good reason. And if the E-

SWAT team had all been wearing gun holsters while tailing Lou, that would've given the game away.

"Are you okay?" Lou repeated, when the woman remained absolutely silent.

No – that wasn't true. Nate could hear her breathing – louder than it should be. Much louder.

Fear.

"She's fine," the shithead grunted.

"I'd really rather hear that from her," Lou said, sounding absolutely calm and reasonable. She kept her attention on the woman only, as if the behemoth of a man was utterly irrelevant to her.

The mop of blonde hair lifted, and the woman met Lou's gaze.

She said nothing, but her message was clear: *Help me.*

Then her head dropped down again.

"Tell her you're fucking fine, Fiona. You can at least fucking do that for me."

Fiona didn't move.

Nate realised she was wearing business attire: a striped pencil skirt, navy blue blouse, sensible heels. A security pass hung from a lanyard at her neck.

Fiona had been at work before the shithead had come along. Did she even know the guy?

He needed to call in backup to meet them at the next station. He was fairly sure he could take the guy down if necessary, but it wasn't at that point yet. The best thing to do would be to get the guy off the train, and Fiona safe.

Ideally peacefully and without freaking out everyone on the train. And that would be easier with backup.

The train took a turn, and the carriage swayed slightly. The tension in the small space was thick, with all passengers' eyes on them: a couple of lanky teenage boys, a middle-aged woman with a thick paperback novel on her lap, and a slightly overweight guy in a suit, probably between meetings.

The suit met Nate's gaze: *should we do something?*

Nate nodded and immediately changed plan. Everyone on the carriage was already freaked out. It was only a few more minutes until Subiaco station, but he could at least let them know the police were onto this. He reached into his back pocket for his police ID.

At the same time, Luella placed a hand on Fiona's shoulder, the one furthest from the brooding man mountain.

"It's okay, Fiona, I'm – "

But whatever Lou was about to say was forgotten as the shithead suddenly reached for the small of his back. Instantly, Nate knew what the guy was doing and he made a grab for Lou, hooking onto the waist of her jeans and yanking her towards him.

At the same time, he activated his mic and spoke in a low, urgent tone as the man began to yell and Fiona screamed.

"One suspect, armed, middle carriage. Black clothing, neck tattoo. Multiple hostages. Approaching Subiaco station."

That was all he had time for before the shithead waved a handgun – a Glock – in the air, as he pulled Fiona back against his chest, his thick ropey arm clamping across her waist.

Nate attempted to tug Lou behind him, but she shoved at the arm that still held her jeans. "Let me go!" she hissed.

"You want to help, you nosy bitch?" the shithead said to Lou. "I'll tell you how you can help."

The man raised the gun until its muzzle pressed against Fiona's temple. The woman whimpered.

Everything in Nate's training told him to remain still. To remain calm. Lou knew all this too.

Yet he could feel her tension and frustration at her helplessness.

He felt it too.

The instant he'd seen that gun, he'd decided he wasn't revealing who he was to this shithead. He wasn't revealing his training, or Lou's training. Who knew where this would lead, but being underestimated could only be a good thing.

His gut feeling was that this guy wasn't about to shoot Fiona. Yet. He wanted something.

"Call the police. Triple zero, whatever," the shithead said. "Call them and tell them I want my fucking kids to be waiting for me by the time we get to Fremantle station, or I'm putting a bullet in someone." He pushed the gun against Fiona's head for emphasis, and she winced. "This cheating whore, or some random on this train. Everyone on this train, even. I don't fucking care."

Someone in the carriage sobbed.

"With my phone?" Lou asked. She was close enough that Nate knew she was shaking – a subtle tremor, but it was there. Her voice revealed none of that.

"Yes, with ya fucking phone. Who else's?"

Lou ignored that, and he watched her fish the phone out of her back pocket, her eyes never leaving the shithead's until she dialled in the emergency phone number: 000.

She swallowed before she spoke. "I'm on a train heading to Fremantle. There is a man here with a gun, who says if his kids aren't waiting at the end of the line, he's going to shoot us."

She paused, briefly looking at the man. "What else should I say?"

"Nothing," he said. "That's enough for now. Bit mysterious, you know?" His grin was disgusting.

Nate could hear the urgent voice of the emergency operator in the absolute silence of the carriage.

"Hang up!" the shithead suddenly barked.

Immediately, Lou pressed the red button that ended the call.

"Good girl," he said, his gaze lecherous as it creeped up and down Lou's body.

The train slowed to a stop at Subiaco station.

The man laughed, an awful, false, villain-ish laugh.

He shoved Fiona's head again with the gun against her temple.

"No one try to get off this train or she dies," he said. Then he looked at the doors and licked his lips. "Good. More hostages."

CHAPTER THREE

THE ONLY PART OF THE PERTH TO FREMANTLE LINE that's underground is Subiaco station. Although it isn't really truly underground, with gaps beneath the curved arches of the roof revealing large slices of a clear blue sky. Lou scanned the platform, which was empty except for a teenager sitting on a bench staring at her phone.

Don't get on this train.

The doors slid open.

Absolutely nobody in their carriage moved.

Their carriage was the middle one of three – the carriage in front would also include the driver, and the carriage behind them was identical to theirs. From glancing through the doors that joined the three carriages, no one had noticed the commotion in their carriage – which wasn't surprising. Not even a minute had passed since the guy had starting waving his gun about like the dickhead he clearly was. People were getting off the other two carriages – good. She wished she could tell the other, oblivious passengers in the carriages to get off too, but she didn't want to risk antagonising the gunman. He'd moved the gun away from Fiona's temple, but his fleshy fingers still gripped that Glock hard, and his vice of an arm hadn't loosened around the woman one bit.

Lou's mind raced as she tried to determine what she should do. She'd never been in a hostage situation before, and she didn't have any negotiator training. Nate probably did, and she was certain he'd already notified E-SWAT through his comms. There was a whole negotiator *team* at Elite SWAT. And snipers and tactical operators who knew exactly how to storm a train. And she'd also just called the police – who in case Nate's comms weren't working or whatever, they also would've called E-SWAT – so help *would* be coming. Soon.

But unless there was a truck full of E-SWAT operators who just happened to be having lunch at one of the many Subiaco restaurants and cafés built immediately above this station, she and Nate were alone for now.

The melodic ding that announced the doors were closing almost made Lou sag with relief. The girl on the bench hadn't moved. No more hostages.

But then, a cavalcade of footsteps heralded a group of people running down the steps to the platform. At the front, a woman in a long skirt with straight black hair.

Behind her were maybe ten more people. Children actually. All girls, in matching uniforms – dresses with green and white checks – a school uniform. A teacher and her students, all maybe twelve or thirteen years old.

"Wait!" the woman with the long skirt yelled out.

No.

The doors were almost shut. One more second and they would be, and the train would be away. The woman and the kids were gathering on the platform. Right near their carriage.

"Wait!" the woman yelled again, waving her hands about in an attempt to capture the driver's attention.

Was it even possible the driver would notice? Did trains have side mirrors? Lou desperately hoped they did not.

Or would the teacher see for herself the danger they were in through the glass doors and windows that provided such a clear view of what was going on inside?

Lou glanced at the guy. He'd dropped the gun by his side. It wouldn't be noticeable from outside. They'd have no idea what they were walking into.

No.

The doors shut fully. Lou held her breath.

Did train drivers ever reopen carriage doors? Lou couldn't remember the last time she'd been on a train, her district was south of Perth, her commute about ten minutes in her little blue hatchback – definitely no need for public transport.

She glanced at Nate. His face was a picture of tension, his gaze entirely focused on the guy and that gun.

Again, the melodic dinging started.

No-no-no-no.

The doors slid open.

Lou turned, and she was immediately facing the teacher and the girls. They were metres away from her, and the moment the doors opened fully, they were going to step onto this carriage and potentially into the line of fire.

The doors were almost open. One girl reached down and absently scratched the side of her calf, the action so normal and *childlike* that it seemed impossible Lou could even contemplate allowing them on the train.

In fact, she couldn't.

"Don't get on the train!" she yelled, although her words were more a screech, and nowhere near as loud as she wanted. "There's a man with a gun!"

For a moment everyone froze – the girls, the teacher, everyone in the carriage.

And then the guy rushed to the open carriage door, dragging Fiona beside him, that gun once again thrust against her head. His thick shoulder bumped Lou hard, and she ricocheted into Nate.

"Pretend it's the wrong train," the man hissed at the teacher. "Pretend *good*, 'cause if this train doesn't leave *now*, someone's getting shot, you understand me?"

The teacher stumbled backwards, waving her arms as if trying to herd a flock of sheep away from the train. But she didn't need to, the girls weren't dumb, they were backing away, step by step.

No one ran, though. No sudden movements.

Just silence, except for the bloody ding of the doors.

"*Pretend!*" the guy hissed, louder.

The woman blinked, then pantomimed a pretty bad rendition of *Oh look! This is the wrong train!* With lots of hand movements and gestures and clearly it somehow worked – as the doors slid shut again.

And as the train finally, *finally* pulled away, the teacher and her students ran back up those steps as if the fires of hell were chasing them.

Lou realised that Nate had wrapped his arms around her after she'd been shoved against him, and now he attempted to pull her behind him as the guy turned his attention to her.

But she wasn't about to cower behind anyone.

"You bitch!" he said. "You fucking interfering little bitch!"

His gun was still held tight in his fist, but at least it was pointed at the ground, not at Fiona, not at her. Not that that was much comfort.

She'd just defied him again, and Lou had no idea what he was going to do now to reassert his sense of control.

Shoot her for disobeying him?

Lou couldn't even let that thought fully form. She couldn't, or she would be absolutely no use to Nate, to the other hostages.

Lou swallowed, her mouth suddenly acrid. She had no idea what to say.

"No one got off the train," Nate said suddenly, his voice a rumble in his chest behind her back. A deep, clear, calm, rumble. "She did what you asked."

"You're going to fucking argue a *technicality*?" the guy said.

"Everyone is doing exactly what you've told them, mate," Nate said. Lou sensed his hesitation before saying *mate* like it was an effort to push the word out. But Nate was being smart, trying to build a rapport with this piece of shit. Trying to stop him from shooting her. "You've already got a train full of hostages, you didn't need any more."

"You some expert in this?" the guy said, his gaze flicking over Nate.

"Nah, mate," Nate said, "But I've got three little sisters. All those girls on here would've been pretty hectic."

Nate didn't have any sisters at all. He had a brother, also a cop. Or at least he had been when she'd been going out with Nate.

The guy almost cracked a smile. "You telling me this nosy bitch did me a favour? You think I'm some kinda idiot?"

"No," Nate said, "I'm just saying that it seems like you have this under control."

Lou couldn't see Nate's face, but knew he hadn't broken eye contact with the gunman. The guy just stared back at Nate, and as Lou watched, she tried to read his thoughts. Poor Fiona was still clamped to his side, although her hair was no longer hanging over her face. Instead she was looking up at him, mascara making greyish tracks down her cheeks. Her gaze was ... pleading.

Pleading for what? To let her go? To put the gun away? To not shoot Lou?

Fear began to overtake the adrenalin that'd been coursing through her veins from the moment this dick dragged Fiona onto the train. Sure, she'd been shocked when he'd drawn his gun. Sure, she'd felt fear when she'd seen those girls on the platform.

But now she felt fear for *herself*. The thought fully formed now, despite all her best efforts:

Was he going to shoot her for disobeying him?

If he wanted to, he could just lift that gun up a bit, and shoot her now. He could shoot Nate, he could shoot Fiona, he could shoot everyone on this carriage. This train.

Fear tightened her throat, settled heavy on her chest.

It would be *so* easy to lean into it, to lean into the fear and let it overwhelm her. But she didn't allow it, she couldn't. She hadn't the last time she'd been in a life and death situation – just two weeks ago – although what good it did her then. But then, at least, she'd had a gun.

Although – again – for what good it did her.

Rather than leaning into the fear, Lou leaned back into Nate's chest, and his arm around her grew tighter. She could feel his heartbeat, its rhythm steady and strong. He was warm, *hot* really, against the thin cotton of her singlet, and in pretty much any other situation being so completely pressed against his body – back, hips, butt – would've been ... something else. Intimate. Sexy.

But right now, of course it wasn't. It wasn't about Nate being a man and her being a woman, or about their history, as ancient as it was.

It was his strength and hers.

Together.

NATE KEPT his attention on the shithead, trying to hide the fact he literally wanted to rip the arsehole's head off. How *dare* he do this? How dare he create the terror in this carriage that was so intense Nate could almost taste it.

Beyond the gunman the other passengers sat in two different rows of seats – the teenage boys right at the back, near the door to the adjacent carriage behind them. The grey-haired woman sat about four rows in front of them, pressed up hard against the window, as if she was hoping she could exit the bloody train by osmosis. The office guy still stood awkwardly gripping the yellow pole near the seats meant for the disabled, his gaze on Nate, as if Nate had some plan.

Which he didn't, really, other than stopping this arsehole from shooting Lou.

He'd had no idea the school kids had been on the platform, his attention entirely on the guy's gun from the moment he'd seen it – his whole body itching with anticipation – because if the shithead gave him an opening, he was taking him down.

So yeah, he hadn't seen the kids, not until Lou started yelling.

And, fuck, he knew that Lou hadn't really had any option. No way should those kids have been allowed on this train. But, still ... this guy already hated her for simply asking Fiona if she was okay. Now she'd gone and painted a red target on her chest.

And if he'd just fucked this conversation up, the shithead was going to shoot her to prove to the carriage – the negotiators, *everyone*, that he decided what happened on this train.

The arsehole's gaze shifted from Nate's, down to Lou. As Nate watched, the man's fingers flexed against the Glock's grip – loosening, then tightening again.

Nate swallowed, his throat dry.

Via the tiny receiver in his ear, he could hear the E-SWAT team relaying their progress. It was less than ten minutes to the next station, which was being evacuated. So were the rest along the line. But there wasn't enough time for an E-SWAT team to get into position at the next stop – not that they'd worked out what to do yet. They needed more intel from Nate first:

What do you reckon he'd do if we stopped the train?

How many hostages?

Can you get him onto a phone? Negotiator is ready.

Obviously, Nate didn't say a word.

The instinct to drag Lou behind him, ignoring her

resistance, was near overwhelming. But he couldn't. He was supposed to be being calm and reasonable. He was supposed to be building a rapport with this piece of shit, not escalating the situation.

So, he remained still, although it just about killed him to do so. The shithead's gaze finally slid back to Nate's.

Something had changed in that gaze. Now it gleamed like he'd just discovered his shit didn't stink.

Nate's arms tightened hard around Lou. She didn't move at all, and he realised she was holding her breath.

He was holding his breath too. His heart beat hard against her back.

"I *do* have this under control," the shithead said finally. "Fucking *everything* is under control."

The gun that Nate hadn't stopped staring at shifted in the man's grasp. His finger curled around the trigger, slowly – like a caress. But just as Nate's muscles bunched, just before he launched himself as that arsehole – no fucking way was he waiting for Lou to be shot, for *him* to be shot – his finger lifted from the trigger.

The shithead turned his head, his attention now on the rest of the hostages. As if he and Lou were forgotten. As if time hadn't just stood still.

Only then did Lou sag against him in relief, and start breathing again. Only when the gunman couldn't see her – couldn't see how much he'd scared her.

Nate would bet everything he owned, everything he *knew*, that Lou had kept her gaze steady – her gaze *brave*

– the whole time that arsehole had been working out whether or not to shoot her.

She craned her neck to look up at Nate, and just fleetingly – like for a nanosecond – he let himself enjoy holding Luella Brayshaw in his arms again, to have her look up at him with softness in her gaze.

Not hurt. Not betrayal.

Predictably, the shithead ended that infinitesimally brief moment with an ugly, brutal shout. "Hey!" he yelled, at the teenagers. They were both tall with narrow shoulders and too long hair. One was in a flannel shirt, the other a white T-shirt printed with the name of a band Nate had never heard of. "One of you go tell the driver no stopping 'til he gets to Freo. If ya not back in a couple of minutes, I shoot the other one of you. And if the train fucking stops, I shoot you both. Got it?"

Both boys nodded, and then both started talking furiously to each other, working out who would leave – even temporarily.

Nate was still staring at that gun. If the shithead turned his back entirely, Nate could possibly go for it.

The thing was, the guy's finger was still near the trigger. There was far too high a risk of the Glock discharging in the process. And, should Nate somehow fail at disarming the guy, there was a pretty good chance he'd be dead. Or someone else on the train would be.

"Go fucking *now*!" the shithead suddenly roared.

This silenced the boys, and one with lank red hair stood and lurched for the door that linked this carriage to the next one. He shoved his palm against the door release and left the carriage.

The door slid shut with such a normal, everyday, innocuous sound it was rather anticlimactic. As if the boy had just gone to sit elsewhere, not gone to absolutely guarantee that this nightmarish train trip was going to continue right to the end of the train line.

No one was getting off until Fremantle.

CHAPTER FOUR

THEY WERE PROPERLY IN SUBURBIA NOW, THE TRAIN winding its way through the leafy, affluent eastern suburbs of Perth, the surrounding architecture a mix of renovated century-old cottages and bleeding edge modernity.

The sky outside was still a perfect, cloudless, blue.

Lou hugged herself, rubbing her hands up and down her bare arms, although the cool of the air conditioning was definitely the least of her problems.

She sat beside Nate, in the part of the carriage where a row of seats backed against each opposing wall of the train, only blue patterned carpet between them. The other passengers were all in the conventional row part of the carriage, except for the dude in a suit who now perched uncomfortably on one of those foldable seats for the disabled. As if even now he thought he shouldn't be using it.

Not that he'd had any choice, the gunman had just directed them all to sit where he told them, and so now Nate and Lou had the not-at-all pleasure of sitting immediately across from him and Fiona. Fiona, finally, was no longer clamped to the guy's side – although he still crowded her, his legs in that classic manspreading pose, forcing Fiona to squeeze her knees together and angle her legs away. His hip still pressed against the woman's, and when she'd try to put even the smallest gap between them he'd said: *don't fucking move.* And that had been that.

The sound of a door sliding open announced the return of the redheaded teenager, his skin polar white beneath his freckles.

Beyond him in the adjacent carriage, the handful of passengers now knew very clearly what was going on, and they all now sat at the absolute furthest seats from this carriage. Lou knew from a quick glance at the carriage behind them that the passengers in that one had done the same. She was absolutely certain that each carriage would be in police contact now, although she imagined that wouldn't be particularly reassuring for them.

Still, better than being in *this* carriage, anyway.

Not that Lou wished herself off this train.

Yes, sure, about two minutes ago when she'd seriously thought she was going to get shot? Yeah, she was pretty damn keen to get off this train.

But now, nope. Not until Fiona and everyone else on this train was safe.

And achieving that would be a shit tonne easier if she could actually talk to Nate. If they could actually form a plan.

She glanced at the man beside her.

He wasn't exactly sprawled on his seat, but he had relaxed back against the patterned fabric, one arm stretched out along the back of the chairs behind her shoulders.

Her shoulders in contrast were stiff, her posture straight. It seemed crazy that just minutes ago she'd been wrapped in his arms, but now she didn't want to touch him. She didn't have time to analyse why – maybe because of what happened a decade ago and she was still pissed at him? Probably. Or maybe because in that moment after the gunman had made his decision not to shoot her – at least not right now – it had felt pretty damn remarkable to be wrapped in his arms?

No. That wasn't it.

But she didn't have time to think about any of that, anyway – of Nate and her, or anything related to how she felt about seeing him again. She kind of needed to focus on the fact she was being held fucking hostage on a train.

Her phone rang.

It was the most boring ringtone available on the far from latest model phone, and it was loud. She'd turned the volume up when she'd been dropped off at Elizabeth

Quay what now felt like hours ago. No way had she been missing a call from Sergeant Peters.

But now, the rhythmic *brrriinngggg* was obscenely loud in the silent carriage. It was as if they'd all been waiting for something to happen.

This phone call was likely it.

"Should I answer it?" Lou asked, hating herself for even pretending to respect his authority.

His smile stretched over his teeth and he nodded approvingly at her.

She kept her shudder on the inside. *Ugh.*

"Yes," he said. "*Please* could the nosy bitch answer her phone."

She'd moved her phone to her front pocket when she'd sat down, but she still had to stand to fish it out of the stiff denim. She swiped to accept the private phone number.

"Hello?" she asked.

But before she even heard the response, the gunman had ripped her phone from her hand. Even that brief touch of his skin against hers made Lou recoil, and she retreated automatically, falling back into her seat when the back of her legs hit the row of chairs behind her.

She met Nate's gaze for a moment, but she couldn't read much in it. Certainly, none of what she glimpsed when she'd been in her arms before. In that moment, he'd been the Nate who'd held her a million times before. Who'd gazed at her like that – with such intensity, such emotion ...

Although the emotions years ago had been more about lust and, and ... well, she'd later learnt it had only ever been lust. Nothing more. But the emotions in his arms on the train had been more along the lines of: *thank fuck we're both alive.*

Which was pretty understandable.

"About time," the gunman said into her phone, dragging her attention back to the rather more pressing life-threatening situation they were in. "You going to go get my kids for me?"

He stood back over his side of the train, tapping the barrel of his gun against his jean-clad thigh as he talked.

The whole train focused on the gunman as he listened to whatever the negotiator was saying. The guy in the suit, the lady with silver hair in a French roll, and the two teenagers still right at the back. And Fiona too, her gaze never wavering from the ugly angles of the man's face.

Fiona had kind of, *unfurled*, now he wasn't touching her. No longer were her spine curving her into the smallest space possible. She'd straightened her shoulders, lifted her chin. And that never-wavering gaze pointed at the gunman? It was filled with hate. With fury.

Suddenly the guy laughed, just a single bark of sound. He looked to Fiona, paying no attention to her hatred.

This was unsurprising. He didn't give a shit what Fiona thought of him. He just wanted to control her. To have her *fear* him.

As if testing he still had both of those things: control and fear – he wagged the gun almost casually in Fiona's direction.

She shrunk back against the wall.

Another disgusting bark of laughter.

But Fiona's head didn't drop this time.

"They wanna know my *name*, babe," he said, talking to Fiona in an approximation of a jovial tone. "Can't find our kids without my name! Would've thought they'd work that out themselves by now, you know, big brother watching and all that." He surveyed the roof of the carriage, presumably searching for CCTV cameras. There were none. Many trains had them in Perth, but not all.

This, it would appear, was considered a low-risk train.

Ha ha.

"My name's Brent," the guy said into the phone, "Brent Carey."

His name was so normal, but Lou wasn't sure what she expected. "Violent Prick" probably didn't appear in any baby name book.

"My kids are Tameka and Rex," he continued. "But fuck knows what school they go to, *this* stupid bitch doesn't let me know details like that. Like, I'm their fucking *dad* and she's made it so I can't even go to their assemblies and shit. Like, what the fuck?" He paused, and then shoved the phone at Fiona.

"Tell them what school they go to. And don't make

shit up, all right? You know I'll shoot one of these hostages if you do, don't you?"

Fiona's gaze slid to Lou's for a second. In her gaze was years of Brent's abuse, and also an awful, resigned acceptance. Yes. Fiona absolutely believed he was capable of shooting someone.

Fiona took the phone. "South Fremantle Primary School," she said, not much louder than a whisper.

Again, Carey's awful smile stretched his lips. "Now isn't that convenient," he said. He grabbed the phone back.

"No excuse for them not to be at Fremantle station waiting for me, you got that?" his voice spat into the phone. "My kids better be on that platform when we arrive, or I'm gonna start shooting." He turned his head to look right at Lou. Just as she had this whole time, she stared right back. Steady, and strong, even as fear slithered down her spine. "And I know exactly who I'll shoot first."

You know I'll shoot one of the hostages.

Nate turned that sentence over in his brain.

Because Fiona *did* know. And not just 'knew' because Carey had probably hit her for years and he was a vicious bastard. She *knew* knew.

He'd killed someone before.

It was Oscar Shepherd in his ear now. His closest mate at Elite SWAT, and one of the sergeants. He was leading the E-SWAT team that would be waiting for them at Fremantle station, and was on the way there now, relaying information as he received it, the sirens on the E-SWAT SUVs a constant in the background.

"He's on bail," Oscar said. "Drug possession. Couple of kgs of meth. He's got court this week, looking at a good stint in the bin."

Carey had taken a few steps away from the hostages, still tapping that Glock against his thigh as he talked to the negotiator.

"He's refused a deal, wouldn't give the detectives anything, and the drug squad couldn't even trace the ice to a known batch. Looks like everyone thinks he has bikie links, but no one's ever heard of him, and there's nothing linking him to a gang. So, a dead end there."

Nate assessed Carey. Was he a member of one of Western Australia's OMCGs - outlaw motorcycle gangs? Was that how he'd come to shoot someone? He certainly had the look of hired muscle, of a standover man. All grunt, no brains.

"His firearm's not his – no registered gun license, never had one," Oscar continued.

No surprises there.

"He's subject to a VRO for a Fiona Carey, who we guess is the woman he's got with him. There are years of call-outs to domestic violence incidents associated with her, but looks like nothing stuck. There's a VRO for the two kids, too, they're eleven and twelve, and they told the social workers during a custody hearing they're scared of him and don't want to see him."

Again, no surprises there. In Nate's experience, mothers who refused access to their kids generally had very good reasons. Usually just the one, actually: protecting their kids from getting hurt by their violent shit of an ex-partner.

"Nate, mate, are you able to tell us anything? How many in your carriage? What's your take on the guy? What are we dealing with here?"

It was driving him insane not being able to communicate with his team. What he did – what Elite SWAT did – was all about teamwork, all about communication.

He couldn't help them if he couldn't speak to them.

Nate shifted the hand currently resting along the back of the seat headrests to squeeze Lou's shoulder. She was stiff as a board, and her head immediately swung to meet his gaze. He reached up and scratched his shoulder, right up near his shirt collar – and right near the collar microphone of his comms.

He had no idea if she was familiar with this comms set-up, or if she'd have any idea what he was asking her to do.

She just looked at him for a moment, as if trying to interpret the message in his eyes. Her eyes were more green than blue in the sunlight that flooded through the windows, her gaze intense and her brow slightly furrowed.

Then she nodded, almost imperceptibly and turned away.

Another few moments later, she coughed.

Just a single cough, giving him a second.

Then, as she started coughing in earnest her hands covering her mouth, Nate leaned towards her, resting a hand on her back as if comforting her, activated his microphone, and talked fast and low.

"Five hostages, plus me and Brayshaw. Nil injuries. Suspect is agitated, and I reckon he's serious about this."

That was all he had time for. Lou had only coughed long enough to give him time to relay a short message, not so long as to piss Carey off.

All Carey did was glare in their direction, then refocus on the phone. Still totally clueless he had a couple of cops as hostages.

He had to force himself to not crack a smile, with Carey looking right at them. But Carey couldn't see Lou's face as she turned towards Nate, and her lips quirked into a grin, her eyes sparkling.

Fuck, Nate thought.

He'd missed that smile.

Lou looked away.

It felt good to work with Nate, to work as a team, even on something as small as creating a distraction so he could send a message to E-SWAT. But she couldn't grin at him like an idiot, and she definitely shouldn't be enjoying just gazing at him.

Like, *time and place,* Luella. Time and place!

The stomp of Carey's feet approaching behind her certainly refocused her on the seriousness of this situation.

Lou swivelled in her seat as he walked back to his side of the carriage, again crowding Fiona as he thumped down onto the seat closest to her. He then dropped Lou's phone on the chair beside him.

Through the windows behind Carey and Fiona, Lou watched the century-old cream stone structure of Claremont station slide by – although not all that quickly. She imagined that driver had been asked to drive slower than normal, to give the E-SWAT team maximum time to get to the end of the line. If Carey had noticed, or even cared, he gave no indication.

How much longer until they made it to Fremantle? Ten minutes? Fifteen?

Lou glanced at the station map painted on the carriage wall above Carey and Fiona. Claremont station was around the half way point, so—

"What's the deal with you two, then?" Carey said, interrupting her thoughts. His tone somehow both friendly and aggressive.

Lou blinked, glancing at Nate.

"How do you mean, mate?" replied Nate, all casual. His arm was still slung across the back of Lou's seat, but she could feel the tension radiating from his body.

"You know," Carey said. "What's the trouble in paradise?"

Lou had no idea what he meant.

Carey tilted his head to look at Fiona. "At least I wasn't dumb enough to marry this," he said, and then laughed like he'd made a joke. Fiona held his gaze resentfully – she was clearly only giving him her attention because it was better than getting shot. Which was smart, but Lou could only begin to imagine how many times Fiona had done what Carey wanted just to placate him.

Lou didn't need another reason to hate Carey, but imagining even a hint of what he'd put Fiona through certainly made the list even longer.

Carey's attention flicked back to Lou, and she held her body stiffly as he stared at her, his gaze shifting down her body in a way that made her feel ill. "But!" Carey suddenly announced gleefully. "The nosy bitch isn't wearing a ring! I got it all wrong. She's not your missus then. Ha! What is she then? Just some slutty hook up piece of arse?"

Nate was up and a step across the carriage before Carey pointed the gun straight at him. He froze instantly.

"Probs not the time to defend her honour, dontcha think big guy?" Carey mocked. "Now sit the fuck down again, *mate*."

For a moment, a moment that was *way* too long, Nate just stood there. Lou reached out and brushed her fingers against his arm, her heart hammering against her chest.

What are you doing, Nate?

"Nate ..." she began, although she had no plan as to what to say next.

But she didn't need to – because of her, or more likely because of the gun still pointed at him – Nate backed off, and dropped slowly back into his seat. He didn't look at Lou at all, but his profile was hard, his jaw tense.

"So, you like her," Carey continued, swinging the gun slightly to point briefly at Lou and then back to Nate. "That must be complicated. A wife *and* a girlfriend." He shook his head. "You're keen. So, what's with the tension? You had a lover's quarrel or somethin'?"

Lou barely acknowledged the question, her gaze immediately drawn to the only reason Carey would think Nate was married.

But, *surely* he wasn't. Surely, she would've noticed before now?

Although to be fair, it'd been less than fifteen minutes, and they'd been held hostage for about thirteen of them. Whether Nate was wearing any jewellery hadn't been a high priority.

But now it was.

And with a simple glance, she saw exactly what Carey had seen.

A simple band, in silver or titanium or white gold or something.

On the ring finger of his left hand.

Nate Rivers was married.

CHAPTER FIVE

No.

No.

No.

Lou was *not* going to be bothered by this.

She was *not*.

She still had a gun pointed at her. That should be all that mattered.

But Nate had gotten married. To someone else.

Lou attempted to swallow away the sudden vice-like grip on her throat, and wish away the lead that had sunk in her stomach.

Neither of those things worked.

She just kept staring at that damn ring, trying to manage her expression. She didn't want Carey to see her shock, not that there was any chance of him guessing the truth.

Hey, I just realised you're both cops who went out for

a few months until one of you said you were in love, and that freaked out the other one who then disappeared forever. And you hadn't seen each other for more than ten years until about fifteen minutes ago, and also – seems like the nosy bitch never really got over you, hey, big guy?

Yeah, no. That wasn't going to happen.

But regardless, no way was the gunman seeing how Lou really felt right now. He was *not* going to see her shock, and hurt and, and …

Oh, damn, she didn't even know how she felt. She just knew this felt bloody awful, and way too much like it had felt to wait for that text or phone call that never came. To feel so stupid, so naïve. So clueless.

To think she'd imagined all if it. The connection. The love.

All of it.

What had been – and even more humiliating still *remained* – the most intense relationship of her life, had been one-sided. There she was imagining a future with Nate, and he was imagining nothing more than how fast he could get her out of her clothes.

And look, she'd been totally into the *getting out of the clothes* part of their relationship too. Totally into it.

With Nate, sex had just been electric. Kissing him had been electric. All of it. His touch, his breath against her skin, his mouth against hers, his cock inside her.

He'd had such power over her, simply by how he made her feel.

And here she was all these years later, still under his

spell. Still capable of being hurt by a man who'd never given a shit about her. And who'd clearly moved on with someone who he *did* give a shit about.

Who he loved.

Lou looked up at Carey.

She'd been planning to say: *We're tense because you're holding us hostage, you arsehole* (probably without the arsehole bit), when Nate spoke.

"She's my ex," Nate said. "It *is* complicated. You know, unfinished business."

Lou's gaze swung up to catch Nate's.

Unfinished business?

What did that mean?

Something shifted in his gaze, and instantly she got it – and that totally unwarranted flame of ... something. Hope? *Ugh*. Anyway – it was extinguished before it even had a chance to flicker.

Nate was back to trying to build a rapport with this guy. Keep him calm. Keep him relaxed.

Which was sensible. *So* sensible. Much more sensible then her urge of only seconds ago to be a smart-arse. But, it appeared that even in the most dire of circumstances, Nate messed with her head.

She'd been wise to not allow herself to even think about him in all these years. To halt her fingers before she was tempted to type his name into the Facebook search bar, and to bite her tongue when she met anyone stationed in the district where Nate had worked and not ask about him. Although maybe if she had, she would've realised he was at Elite SWAT, and she wouldn't have run away from him like an idiot at Perth train station.

"I know all about complicated exes, big guy," Carey said, relaxing his arm so the gun no longer pointed straight at them but instead somewhere on the carpet. "What she do to you?"

Another station passed by through the carriage windows; Lou had no idea which one. How close were they to Fremantle? What would be waiting for them when they got there?

Nate cleared his throat, and Lou noticed his hands flex slightly against the tailored fabric of his trousers. After his lie about having three sisters, what story was he going to concoct now?

"Nothing," Nate said, his tone flat. "She didn't do anything wrong."

"Pardon me?" she said, before she could stop herself.

Nate looked down at her, the first time since the gun had appeared that it wasn't in his line of sight. "You didn't do anything wrong," he repeated. His gaze was strong, direct. *Real.*

She didn't know what to do with those words, so she just turned them over in her brain.

"Yes, she *did*," Carey suddenly said, his words sharp and loud. "They always do. Especially bitches like that one."

Lou looked at Carey, and as she did, a cloud passed over the sun or something, and he was momentarily in shadow. But even when he was back in the generous sunlight, the darkness still remained – everything about this man was hard and dark. From his black boots to his dark hair, to the awful, hateful glint in his eyes.

The man beside her felt like a coiled spring of muscle, and so she pressed her knee against his, just for a second, trying to tell him: *It's okay. He's not worth it.*

As if she cared what this piece of shit thought or said about her.

"I did, actually," Lou said. "I wanted more from him than he was willing to give."

The train swayed around a curve, and Nate's shoulder pressed against hers for a long moment.

Carey rolled his eyes and looked at Nate. "I know what that's like," he said. "This one," he nodded at Fiona, who was staring again at the floor. "Wanted to get married, but I didn't. Then she fell pregnant and I stuck around. Supported her. You know?" He shook his head, just as Fiona lifted hers so she could look at him. "And what do I get for that? One day she just packs everything up and leaves. Gets the police involved, like she thinks I'd hurt her. And she *knows* I'd never hurt her or the kids ..."

There was a long pause as Carey turned his attention to Fiona, as if drawn by the hatred in her gaze. His look was just as hateful, but it was a totally different flavour of hate. Fiona hated Carey for all he must have put her through, and for what he was doing to her now. But Carey's hate wasn't really about Fiona. The same hatred defined everything he did – the exact same hate was in his gaze when he looked at Lou.

He was fuelled by hate and the sense of entitlement that underpinned it.

Lou predicted his next words long before he said them.

"She knows I'd never hurt her or the kids," he repeated, "for no reason."

For no reason.

And with those simple words, he'd justified every violent action of his entire relationship, and most likely his entire life.

CAREY'S THREATENED *to shoot a hostage if we call him back before Fremantle station.*

Keep him calm, keep him talking. If he's calm and talking, he's not shooting people.

A fat fucking lot of good Oscar's directions had done Nate when Carey called Lou a slut. He'd seen red.

A very specific shade of red: Carey's blood red, splattered all over the clear glass windows after Nate had smashed his face in.

But now, Nate pressed his knee against Lou's, and not because the train had taken a curve or anything.

They'd been having a bit of a conversation with their knees and shoulders these last few minutes: First Lou trying to calm him down when he'd wanted to leap across the train ... *again.* But how stupid would he have to be to launch himself at an armed arsehole a second time?

To do it once had been incredibly stupid. Incredibly

negligent given he was the mostly highly trained person in this carriage, and he could've easily pushed Carey over the edge.

He'd *never* acted so impulsively on a job before. He was a tactical operator: everything he did was carefully planned and executed. To behave the way he had was unacceptable.

And yet he'd almost done it again, until the touch of Lou's leg against his had pulled him back together. Grounded him.

Later he'd bumped her shoulder to tell her ... what? To thank her for going along with this conversation? Or to tell her that she hadn't been wrong at all to want more all those years ago?

It was more the second option, Nate suspected.

She'd just been wrong to want it with him.

But just now, he'd needed to touch her because he'd needed to do what she'd done for him: ground her. Keep her focused on this tightrope of a reality they currently stood upon, and not be distracted by ancient memories that could have them *all* falling to their deaths.

And, look, all of these things were *really* not appropriate to be concerning himself with on a moving train with an angry gunman and seven hostages. He shouldn't be thinking about Lou, or their past, her past, or *anything* except keeping the shithead calm.

He needed to get them *all* to Fremantle station safely, and then E-SWAT could end this.

Would end this.

Yet it still burned to just sit here and let Carey talk shit. Shit that definitely hurt Fiona, who sat beside Carey in a mass of fear and fury; and also hurt Lou.

But just sit here, he did. He swallowed and committed to what he needed to do.

"That sucks she left, mate," Nate said. "What happened after that?"

Out of the corner of his eye, he watched Fiona's jaw drop open, and her eyes widen with shock and hurt.

I'm sorry, he thought, *this is negotiation 101: empathy and open-ended questions.*

But he couldn't even look at her. He needed Carey to believe this.

Carey's forehead wrinkled. "Why do you give a fuck?"

Nate shrugged. "You must have your reasons for being here today," he said. "I'm curious."

"You want to know why I'm going to shoot you?"

Another whimper from the lady with the book, seated only metres away to his left. The other four hostages had been absolutely silent since Subiaco station until now.

Shhh, Nate thought. *Let Carey focus on* me, *not you.*

Carey's eyes gleamed with satisfaction. He loved all of this: the control, the fear.

"You haven't shot anybody," Nate said. "You haven't hurt any of us."

Downplay the hostage taker's actions so far. Focus on the positives.

"You don't think I'll do it?" Carey said, leaping to his feet and raising the gun again. Nate stared at the Glock pointed straight at his head.

Fuck, fuck, fuck.

He was no negotiator, and he scrambled for what he remembered from long-ago basic training, and Oscar's half heard guidance in his ear from earlier, which he'd been unable to concentrate on with Carey talking and *pointing a gun at him* and all.

Nate's pulse thumped in his ears. He *needed* to get this right.

"I think you want to see your kids, and I think you know if you shoot me now that might not happen," he said.

Carey shrugged. "I'd have six more hostages just in here," he said. "Plus, the other two carriages. Still heaps of leverage."

But his gun fell back to his side. He didn't sit though, instead he walked away – over to the other hostages.

He didn't say a word, and neither did the hostages. He just walked up the aisle between their seats, stood for a second beside each of them: the office guy, the lady with the book, and the teenagers, and then slowly, slowly walked back. Again, pausing hostage by hostage. The carriage was perfectly silent, except for the creak and sway of the train and the heavy, muffled sound of Carey's boots on the carpet.

Carey was revelling in their fear, loving how they all kept their heads bowed, their bodies curled into the smallest possible targets, holding their breath while he paused beside them.

Wondering if they were going to die.

Carey's smile was disgusting. Everything about the man was disgusting.

And yet Nate just had to sit still, and let this piece of shit cultivate fear.

Finally, Carey stood before Nate again. Nate didn't bow his head.

Neither did Lou beside him.

Another station slid by. Mosman Park, with a row of towering pines behind the couple of benches on the platform. Only a few kilometres until Fremantle now.

Nate kept an eye on the gun, still held casually against Carey's thigh. He knew exactly what Carey was going to do now, but he wasn't going to stop him. Carey's free hand had formed into a fist, and he rubbed his fisted knuckles against the black denim of his jeans.

If he was lucky, *this* would be his opportunity. This would be his chance to grab that gun and end this now.

But he played dumb, trying to relax his face into something neutral. Not give away a hint of what he was thinking, or what he was capable of.

The punch came as expected, and he didn't block it. Instead, as Carey's fist connected with his cheek, he turned and flicked his head away from the punch so it passed through him, rather than hitting him solid.

Still hurt like fuck, but years of boxing training weren't wasted.

As he collapsed away from the punch, and reached for his face as if to protect himself from more blows, his gaze flew to that gun.

It was *so* close.

But he wasn't close enough. Carey had punched him once, and stepped away.

He couldn't take the risk.

Nate gritted his teeth in frustration.

"Knew those were gym muscles, big guy," Carey spat. "Piss weak, you are. But hope it's clear now. I *have* hurt someone, and if you fucking pretend to give a shit about me again, I'm hurting *her* next." Carey jerked his head in Lou's direction. "Fists or bullets next time, big guy?" Carey taunted, his attention back on Nate. "Let's wait and see."

Then he sat back in his seat, far too close to Fiona, his legs spread wide, his finger caressing the Glock's trigger.

Behind him, they passed another station: Victoria Street.

North Fremantle was next, then Fremantle.

They were almost there.

"No one fucking say another word, you got that?" Carey announced to the carriage.

Nate straightened back up in his seat, sliding his hand away from his face, and wiping the blood from where his cheek had split open onto the grey of his trousers.

"And while I'm at it - don't move either." Carey

paused, then said to Lou, "That means you, too, nosy bitch. No kissing him better, no nothing."

Lou didn't move. But she did press her leg hard against his.

Even through the layers of linen and denim, her touch was warm and electric.

Grounding.

Two stops to go.

CHAPTER SIX

THE SOUND OF CAREY'S FIST SMASHING AGAINST Nate's face had made Lou feel sick. Flesh and bone hitting flesh and bone was a brutal, primal noise.

It had taken *everything* in her not to leap to her feet to retaliate.

But common sense had held her still. She knew perfectly well Nate could defend himself. And Carey had telegraphed that punch. No doubt Nate could've blocked it, but he hadn't.

He'd had a strategy. She wished she knew what it was, of course. But it was a strategy.

Maybe as simple as having Carey underestimate Nate. Let him feel cocky, feel invincible.

But ... for what purpose?

With Fremantle station now only minutes away, Lou *hated* how she had no idea what was going to happen next. *Did* Nate have a plan? Was he going to make a move before they got there? Or when they did? Or wait for the E-SWAT team?

Had E-SWAT used his comms to explain their tactics? Was there a grand plan that Nate was part of with Lou remaining a clueless bystander?

Look, she didn't have an issue with the E-SWAT team doing their job. She didn't have any experience in this type of situation, and the last thing she wanted to be was a liability. She didn't need to be part of the – hopefully – peaceful end to all of this, as getting everyone out of here safe was what mattered. Her ego didn't need to give her a starring role.

But. It was infuriating being ignorant. It was infuriating being unable to help.

All she could do was sit here next to Nate while blood stained his shirt and the train rattled and screeched along the tracks, the air thick with fear and tension.

And at the back of her mind, wonder what she was going to do if Carey didn't surrender at the end of the line. Which – to be honest – seemed unlikely.

Would she hold it together this time? Or would she fail when it most mattered, just like she had a fortnight ago? When the stakes had been at their highest, and she'd known *exactly* what she'd needed to do ... but hadn't done it.

She hadn't done it, and someone could've died because of her indecision. *She* could've died.

And that time all she'd had to deal with was a knife, not a gun.

Carey held that gun firmly now. No longer was he holding it casually, like he had at times throughout this journey. His finger rested on the trigger, and he surveyed the carriage with a regular sweep of his gaze as if searching for a potential threat.

The train rumbled past North Fremantle station. Almost there.

Carey straightened in his seat. No more manspreading, no more sprawled posture. His shoulders were straight, and he was bouncing one leg rapidly up and down on the spot. He was a ball of tension, but also of ...

Lou attempted to interpret Carey's expression surreptitiously. The gleam in his eyes and the slight curve to his lips were certainly not about fear. He *wanted* to get to the station. He wanted what was going to come next.

It wasn't fear building for Carey as they approached Fremantle station.

It was anticipation.

Lou swallowed, and dug her fingernails into the palm of her hand.

She just needed to keep it together. She just needed to remain calm, and rational, and that way she'd be of most help to Nate, and the E-SWAT team – and to every single hostage on this train.

She closed her eyes for a second, her fingernails pressing harder into the skin of her palm – as if she was trying to make this all feel more real. As if she needed to feel *more* in this moment, a moment that couldn't feel any more real, or any more significant.

Her eyes popped open to find Carey looking straight at her.

He didn't say a word, but over his shoulder the familiar icons of Fremantle appeared: The mammoth container ships with their rainbow of building-block like containers; and the elegant, towering reach of the giraffe-like cranes that stretched to the perfect clear sky above the deep blue depths of the harbour.

They'd arrived.

Lou kept eye contact with Carey as the train slowed – knowing it was probably dumb, but unable to allow herself to submit to him – to submit even to his gaze. Around them, the passing landscape eventually ground to a halt, and the train's wheels gave a high-pitched squeal as they grabbed hard onto the tracks.

Then, it was silent.

The platform was behind Lou, and in front of her was nothing but Carey, Fiona, and a couple of empty sets of tracks.

She couldn't see a soul.

But of course, they were there.

Somewhere, an E-SWAT team lurked. And more police. A negotiator. Probably a sniper or two. Medics.

Carey knew it too. He smirked, or maybe leered – Lou couldn't be sure – everything the man did was just ugly to her.

Her phone rang.

Carey had left it on the seat beside him, but he maintained eye contact for too many more long seconds before finally reaching for his phone – and then Lou was able to take the breath she'd had absolutely no idea she'd been holding.

"Where's my kids?" he barked, immediately.

Lou's gaze flicked to the other hostages. They'd all shifted slightly, and no longer appeared to be attempting to hide in their seats. They all looked ready to leap to their feet, probably partly a product of the tempting proximity of the platform and freedom – but more likely mostly about being ready to *do something* once whatever was going to happen, happened. Run, duck, hide ... who knew? But something.

Because something was definitely going to happen. Soon. The air crackled with it.

"Bullshit," Carey snapped. "They should be here by now."

He glared at Fiona, who shook her head. "Think about it, Brent," she said, her voice soothing, "we've only been on the train twenty minutes. No way they've got them both out of class, and into—"

The smash of the Glock against the side of her head silenced her – and the next sound she made was the force of her head smacking into the carriage window behind her.

She didn't move at all after that.

Nate grabbed Lou's hand before she'd even realised she was starting to stand.

"*Don't,*" he whispered urgently.

But Carey didn't hear him, he was too busy yelling into the phone.

"Stop fucking trying to *reason* with me, all right? I'm not a fucking idiot. You're probably lying anyway. How do I know you even have my kids?" He stood up and walked all the way up to the empty end of the carriage as the negotiator presumably talked to him.

Suddenly, Carey went still, as if he was considering something.

Then he walked up to the doors between their carriage and the one at the rear of the train and slammed his palm against the button to open them.

Nothing happened.

"You've locked me in?" Carey laughed. "Well then sure, yeah, why fucking not. I'll let those two carriages go if you get Rex on the phone. No skin off my nose. He'll set you straight. And there'll still be plenty of hostages left here to make my point, don't you think?"

Carey pivoted away from the door and walked back over to where Lou and Nate sat.

"But don't open the doors to this carriage, all right? I'm not stupid, I'm not giving you a free shot at me."

He must've meant by removing the barrier of the door. Lou was no expert in glazing or knew much about the capabilities of sniper rifles, but she did know it would be difficult to get an accurate shot through toughened glass.

Across the carriage, Fiona groaned, and her eyes fluttered open. She reached one hand up to feel the back of her head, and then to skim the already purpling bruise on her cheek, smearing the beads of blood that had formed where the Glock had grazed her skin.

Carey completely ignored her and continued to pace up and down the carriage, muttering away to the negotiator.

"Now, don't try anything, you got that? You try to be clever and a hostage dies. Understand?"

Lou watched Carey, now standing beside book lady. Was it deliberate? Standing close to a hostage to make it more difficult for a sniper?

But also – would they even take a shot?

Lethal force *had* to be justified, after all, you've got a hell of a lot of talking to do after using it, so you'd better be bloody sure you're shooting with good reason – or you could be up for murder.

Had Carey done enough to justify a sniper bullet? He'd hit Nate, he'd hit Fiona. But they'd be okay. He hadn't shot anyone. No one had been killed.

Besides, E-SWAT didn't have any vision of the carriage, or two-way comms with Nate. They didn't know exactly what Carey had been doing. Being armed in a way to cause fear was absolutely an offence – but it was punishable by a prison sentence, not death. Exactly the same applied to the offence of threats to kill.

He was undeniably an arsehole, but did that justify killing him?

From a police procedural point of view – and in real

life, not the movies - no, Lou decided. With the information E-SWAT had, not yet.

Without evidence of someone's life being under actual, immediate threat, the E-SWAT team's *only* option was to negotiate this to a peaceful conclusion.

So meanwhile, inside this carriage, Nate and Lou were still on their own.

And in this carriage, Lou still had very little hope that this wasn't going to escalate.

The anticipation that oozed from Carey's every pore was all about violence. *Everything* about the man was about violence. Lou had no doubt that violence was a tool he saw as part of his everyday life. If he wanted something, if he was angry, if he was frustrated ... he'd use violence.

And today he was all those things.

The familiar melodic dings that usually heralded the opening of the carriage doors were loud and out of place in the tense carriage.

Of course, their doors didn't open. But the doors to the other two carriages did, and Lou twisted in her seat to see if there were any police waiting for the hostages.

But the platform was empty, the unoccupied metal bench seats looking so *normal* in a line in front of the red brick station building, no one visible beyond the original, beautiful many-paned windows.

As Lou watched, hostages streamed from the two open carriages. The front carriage passengers headed to the ticket barrier at their end of the platform, while the rear carriage headed for the other ticket barrier, almost directly in front of their centre carriage.

The passengers from the rear carriage were a motley group – three young teenage girls, a few men in business attire, a smartly dressed woman with her arm around an older gentleman as she guided him to the exit. Not one of the hostages carried a bag, and not one hesitated as they fled through the open ticket gates.

They'd clearly been guided by the police – and Lou thought she might have glimpsed the outline of an E-SWAT operator in overalls, ballistic vest, balaclava and helmet amongst the shadows as the hostages entered the station's main hall.

Although whether she saw him or not, she knew they were there.

Waiting.

She glanced at Carey. She'd kept him in her periphery vision as she'd watched the other passengers. He hadn't moved from beside book lady.

She wasn't surprised.

Carey didn't care about the other carriages. He cared about *this* carriage.

He lifted the phone back to his ear. "Get me my son."

So close.

Fuck, how many times did Carey have to walk past Nate but *not quite fucking close enough* for Nate to be certain he could disarm him? Maybe if he hadn't been so bloody stupid before and charged across the carriage at him, the man wouldn't be giving him such a wide berth now?

But regardless, he hadn't got his opening, even though he was searching for it constantly.

In his ear, Oscar had filled him in on the set-up.

A couple of sierras – *snipers* – were stationed some distance away opposite the platform. There wasn't a lot of cover between the railway line and the harbour – just a huge car park where freighter ships dropped off brand new cars from overseas, and a few miscellaneous red-roofed buildings beyond a vacant lot. But the building they'd picked, beyond all of that and on the edge of the harbour, was plenty close enough for the E-SWAT sierras who would have no problems even a kilometre away. And there was another sierra at closer range, hidden within the station building somewhere, who also had his sights on Carey.

But they didn't have an order to shoot. Not yet. But if – *when* – they did, the train's door and window glass were incredibly strong – and would definitely impact the trajectory of the sierras' bullets. Sure, they had special rounds for shooting through glass, but any shot would deviate – and how much wasn't an exact science.

And just like how Nate hadn't taken a half chance (or even an 80 percent chance) on attempting to disarm Carey because of the potential disastrous consequences of an error. This was just as true – *more* true – for the sierras', with so many hostages in here.

The rest of the E-SWAT operators had surrounded the train with a couple of guys just below each carriage door facing out onto the tracks, out of sight, but only metres away.

But they'd decided not to risk boarding when the other hostages had exited, even though Carey hadn't noticed that the rear doors had also been opened along with the platform-facing doors – or that they were still open. But they would board, soon. The team was just waiting for the right moment.

"Rex!" Carey said, into the phone. "You on your way to see me, boy?"

His tone was different – a caricature of sing-song and friendly, but not even close to hitting the mark. Nate bet his son was very familiar with the malice that underlined every word his father said.

They hadn't been able to hear a word of the negotia-tor's side of the phone conversation – but they did hear Carey's son when he spoke. Or rather, shouted. He must have, for his young, strong voice to be so crystal clear.

"Have you hurt Mummy?"

How old had Oscar said Rex was? Twelve? Maybe old enough to have shifted to calling his mother 'mum', not 'mummy'. Old enough to think he was grown up, not a little kid any more.

Yet he'd called her *mummy*, and the fear, anger, accu-sation, and *youth* in his voice was heartbreaking as it reverberated around the carriage.

Nate shifted his attention from the Glock momentarily to glance at Fiona. Carey had hit her hard, and she probably had a concussion from that blow and the subsequent whack against the train window. She'd looked fuzzy and not quite there since she'd woken, but at her son's voice, he saw the determination he'd glimpsed earlier ease back into her body. She was a fighter, this woman. She'd left this piece of shit and rescued her children already. What she was thinking right now was as clear as day: *I am getting off this train and back to my kids*.

The only potential roadblock to this plan was now waving that Glock around as he yelled at his son – the brief pretence of playing happy families obliterated.

"Don't you miss ya dad? Don't you want to see me? It's been over a fucking year that bitch has kept you from me!"

Rex didn't speak loud enough for the silent carriage to hear him, even though they all hung on every word of the conversation. Book lady stared up at him, not even a metre from Carey, her perfectly coiffed grey-blonde hair a jarringly elegant contrast to the brutish thug standing in the aisle.

"Rex? Rex?" Carey said urgently. A pause. "No, I don't want to fucking talk to you right now. I want to talk to my son."

He started walking again. Only a few steps. He paused in front of the guy in the suit. If Nate had been suit guy, Carey would've been close enough for Nate to go for it. This would've all been over in seconds.

But suit guy had his back pressed hard against the gaudy fabric of his chair, his legs twisted the way you do when people need to get past you to get to their seats at the football or a concert or something. He wasn't going to be disarming Carey – not that Nate wanted him too. He didn't need any misplaced heroism on this train. Especially with the E-SWAT guys so close.

"Rear carriage, Smithy's in." Oscar said into his ear.

Nate didn't move a muscle, didn't look, didn't do anything.

"*Five* more minutes? Are you fucking kidding me?" Carey started walking again, his movements jerky and tense. But he was keeping up the other end of the carriage, too far away from Nate.

Someone groaned – probably suit guy, maybe one of the teenagers. At being in this limbo for another five minutes? He needn't worry about that, as Nate thought it was highly unlikely this situation was going to last that long. Carey was a tinder box, and *something* was going to happen soon.

Through his earpiece Nate knew the team was still holding out hope for this to be ended peacefully, for the negotiator to be able to talk Carey off this train.

But Nate didn't see that happening.

It might not be on Carey's record, but this shithead had killed before. And he wanted blood today. Nate felt it in his bones.

The man was angry. He was directing it at Fiona, but was that really it?

Or was there something more to this?

"No!" Carey said. "I gave you two fucking carriages full of hostages. That's enough." The man shook his head as he paced again, his stride even more agitated now. "You really do think I'm stupid, don't you? Think you've tricked me? All those hostages for a fucking *phone call*. I'm giving you shit, and if you keep this up I'm gonna shoot someone." He paused, once again in front of suit guy. If he lifted the Glock, if he pointed it at the hostage, this was ending.

Carey's fingers flexed on the gun's grip, but he didn't raise it from beside his thigh.

"Fridge is in, rear carriage." Oscar's voice was crisp in his ear.

Two armed operators now on the train. Both in the carriage furthest from where Carey now stood. Smithy was experienced, ten years in E-SWAT. Fridge had been in two years, still a newbie in this world, regardless of his almost ten years as an ordinary beat cop before that.

Another *ordinary beat cop* sat beside him, her body a tense mass of energy even as she sat perfectly still. Lou had *always* been like that for him, so intense, so full of *everything*. Determination. Grit. Stubbornness. Lust. *Love.*

She was magnetic – and for so long he'd allowed them to be drawn together, until he'd began to understand that it was up to him to keep them apart.

But, yeah. Nothing ordinary about Luella Brayshaw.

He just knew it was killing her to sit so still, to be so

helpless. Hell, it was how he felt too. But he at least knew what else was going on. He'd do just about anything to tell her what he knew, and even more so: to put his arm around her and tell her everything was going to be all right.

Although he didn't know that, of course.

Everything could still go terribly, terribly, bloody wrong.

"You want a show of fucking good faith?" Carey's voice was edging onto a scream now, well beyond a shout.

Nate knew that the negotiator would be scrambling to dial Carey down, to get him out of this electric, knife-edge of a mood.

But it wasn't going to work, he didn't believe that at all. This wasn't ending with Carey walking off this train.

Suddenly, Carey was on the move again. This time towards him and Lou.

"Fine," he said, flatly, into the phone. "You can have your fucking show of good faith hostage, then I need to see my kids. I *need to see them*. You got it? You got *that*?"

Carey came to a halt, just to the far side of Luella.

"Get up," he said to Lou.

She looked at Nate. *What do I do?*

"That wasn't a question, nosy bitch," Carey said. "Not a fucking question at all."

Oscar was in his ear, urgent and distinct: "We've got new intel from covert ops. This guy *does* have a history of gun violence, so when the door opens, the sierras and the guys on board are ready if he looks like shooting."

Nate nodded, but he didn't like this at all.

If? It wasn't if, it was when.

Lou didn't like it either. He could feel her unease. This didn't feel right – not that anything ever felt right in the middle of a hostage situation – but this *wasn't* right. He could feel it in his gut.

But what were their options? Say no?

Carey's finger rested on the trigger, and he shifted his weight from foot to foot, a jittery mess of activity. Of anger and fury and violence.

Lou stood.

"I'll let you off, so you can stop pissing me off," he said, in an almost jovial tone. Like he and Lou shared a private joke. "Walk to the door," he said.

Lou glanced at Nate as she passed him, her leg brushing against his knees.

Had she done that on purpose? Touched him on purpose?

But that wasn't another reassuring touch. In her eyes Nate could see that she knew this felt off. It felt very, very wrong.

But the E-SWAT team was in place. As soon as that door opened – and the connecting doors between the carriages at the same time Nate guessed – they'd have multiple clean shots on Carey.

Only a few more seconds, and everyone would be safe. *Lou* would be safe.

But right now, she wasn't.

His whole body prickled with awareness, with the

certainty that this wasn't like before. Carey wasn't going to let Lou just walk off the way he'd let the other two carriages of hostages go. He'd picked Lou for a reason.

He hadn't chosen the grey-haired woman, who sat with tears now openly streaming down her face, who posed zero threat to Carey. He hadn't chosen the two teenagers: the two *children* who had their whole lives ahead of them.

He hadn't chosen Nate, who was taller and stronger and the only potential threat that Carey knew about on this train.

He'd chosen Lou.

And despite only minutes ago being adamant that these carriage doors *would not* be opened, Carey no longer cared. He wasn't even hanging back as Lou walked to stand right in front of the doors. He was right there, right beside her.

And then he wasn't.

As the train began its familiar beeping as the door began to open – a sound that now felt anything but benign – Carey took a step back. Lou took a deep breath and straightened her shoulders as she faced the carriage doors and the safety beyond. There she stood: tall and determined, her hair a long rope between her rigid shoulder blades.

Then Carey took another step.

Nate was halfway to his feet as Carey spoke, making Lou jerk her head to hear him, her braid flinging over her shoulder.

"They're never going to let me see my kids, you fucking nosy bitch!" he yelled, the Glock lurching upwards.

And then as Carey fired, Nate threw himself through the air.

CHAPTER SEVEN

GLASS EXPLODED ABOVE LOU AS SHE COLLAPSED TO the carriage floor, showering her in a blizzard of harmless safety glass snow.

Something burned – her shoulder, her neck, her arm? Lou had no idea, and it didn't matter.

She wasn't dead. But she needed to do something, *now*, or Nate might be.

The force of Nate's body propelled Carey against a row of empty seats, both men grunting with the impact.

The gun.

Where was it?

Lou leapt to her feet, as Nate grappled with the smaller man. Nate might have him in height, reach, and skill, but Carey was rabid. He fought Nate with a desperation that seemed almost superhuman, although none of his blows landed as Nate easily ducked and weaved. But both Carey's hands were formed into fists. No gun.

Where was it?

Lou rushed passed the fighting men, her eyes on the ground, trying to guess where the firearm had gone.

"Here!" It was book lady, her voice a stage whisper, as if she didn't want Carey to hear. But Carey was too busy trying to avoid Nate's fists – and failing, as that unmistakeable sound of bone hitting flesh again, then again, sounded behind Lou.

The bloody carriage doors were still dinging: *surely* the doors were open by now?

But it just added to the cacophony: grunts and fists and thumps and dings as bodies smacked against chairs and floor and walls.

The gun lay neatly beside book lady, on top of her book: the lethal chunk of metal incongruous against the embracing couple emblazoned across the romance novel's cover.

Lou reached for the Glock, but the woman placed her hand on top of it. "What are you going to do with it?" she asked, with a narrowed gaze and dried tears covering her cheeks.

"I'm a police officer," Lou said, "and so's he," she added, nodding at Nate, who deftly avoided another misfired punch.

Lou didn't wait for the woman's reply, she just grabbed the firearm and held it easily in her right hand. Despite knowing the residual warmth of the grip was from Carey's touch and sweat, the relief in holding it was visceral: a shiver that swept through her body. She had the gun. And on equal terms, Nate had Carey covered.

This was over.

She turned to face the men, just in time to see Nate land yet another blow that sent Carey clear across the cabin. Fiona snatched her legs upwards as Carey skidded along the floor on his back, then perched her heels on the edge of her chair, her face pale but for the bruise still blooming across her face.

The dings still continued incessantly, and Lou glanced at the doors: still closed, except for the damage done by the bullet – in fact one panel of the door had shattered completely. Nate stood at Carey's feet – talking briskly through his comms, his attention never shifting from the unconscious man at his feet.

Nate sent the briefest look in Lou's direction. "The bullet's done something to the doors, they won't open," he said.

Lou nodded. "I've got the gun," she said, and Nate looked back again, his eyes catching onto hers for longer this time, relief mixed with adrenaline in his gaze.

We did it.

Lou got that, the buzz of satisfaction of getting the bad guy. It was probably primal – good triumphing over evil or something. Whatever it was, it felt damn good. Especially sharing it with Nate. That hadn't happened before, she'd met him at cadet training, she'd never worked with him on the—

A strangled noise cut through the never-ending

dinging as Fiona suddenly threw herself on top of Carey's unconscious body, her arms and legs pumping and kicking as she screamed at him, landing blows wherever she could.

"I hate you!" Her voice broke. "I hate you, I hate you, I hate you—"

Swiftly Nate reached for her. "Fiona, don't—"

But suddenly she wasn't on top of the prone man any more. Her body was yanked from Nate's outstretched fingers, and somehow, in a flurry of activity, her back was pressed against Carey's chest, and the no longer prone man held a flick knife to her throat.

Carey scooted backwards on his butt, then clambered to his feet, the blade opening a thin red line at Fiona's throat as he manhandled her upright.

Lou raised the gun and pointed it right at Carey's head. "Police!" she said clearly. "Drop your weapon!"

That bit was easy. It was instinctive. It was just lifting her arms. Saying the words.

Carey grinned or scowled – it was impossible to tell. "A cop?" he barked. "Of course, you are. But what you going to do now, you nosy bitch? I'm dead anyway, might as well take the woman who ruined everything with me."

Fiona screamed as the blade slid deeper against her skin.

"Drop your weapon!" Lou repeated. "Drop your weapon or I'll shoot!"

The doors still beeped. The gun was still steady in

Lou's hands. She was a good shot, in very close range, and Fiona was much shorter than Carey.

She could do this. She could do this. This wasn't like last time. It wasn't her life at stake, it was Fiona's.

"*Please!*" Fiona begged, as blood dripped down to the notch at the base of her pale neck.

She could do this. It was the *right* thing to do. Lethal force was the *only* thing to do.

She let her finger tighten, just a little and—

Blood and brains and bone exploded all over the carriage wall behind Carey, and everybody started screaming.

Fiona, book lady, suit guy, and the teenagers. Screams and sobs.

But Lou hadn't pulled the trigger.

She turned. Behind her stood two E-SWAT operators, each dressed in their distinctive black overalls, ballistic vest, balaclava, and helmet. Both held their AR-15 rifles. Lou had no idea who had just obliterated Brent Carey's skull.

Neither said a word, but the one closest – who's dark grey eyes and a strip of tanned skin revealed by the balaclava were the only part of him not covered in black – said everything with his gaze.

We couldn't wait.

For Lou to get her shit together and do her job. *To save Fiona's life.*

Finally, finally the beeping ceased, and the doors slid open. Suddenly the carriage was full – with paramedics and more police and who knew what else. There was so much talking, but Lou heard none of it.

And then she was off the train.

She was standing in the original great hall in the train station, with its century-old black and white tiles and sky-high ceilings – and currently home to the operation's command post. A paramedic had blotted up the graze the bullet had burned against her neck, but it was barely a scratch. She didn't even need a bandage.

There were *so* many people in the great hall, so many people talking to her, checking her over, asking if she was okay.

Lou had no idea what she said.

She just knew that Nate was with the rest of the Elite SWAT team, and she was on her own. Standing awkwardly and pathetically, just as she deserved.

She'd fucked up. Again.

A touch on her arm made her jump. Nate.

"We need to go back to HQ to debrief," he said. He stood so close to her, far closer than was absolutely necessary. She didn't tilt her chin to look up at him, instead she glared at the threads that were all that remained of the buttons that had been ripped off during his fight with Carey.

Lou nodded. Her throat was tight and raw with frustration. She felt incapable of speech.

Incapable of pretty much anything.

Like the masochist she was, her gaze drifted to his

wedding ring. Like she needed an additional kick in the guts right now, but hey, there it was.

She'd almost let a woman die in front of her, and she was still sulking like a teenager girl about Nathan Rivers.

She *was* pathetic.

"Hey," Nate said gruffly, "Can we talk later? I—"

"No," she said crisply and rubbed at her arms, even though it wasn't cold in the slightest. "Let's get back to HQ."

ELITE SWAT HQ was just outside the city. Nate sat beside Lou in the back of one of the unmarked SUVs as Oscar drove away from Fremantle. They headed down Stirling Highway, the Indian Ocean perfect and navy blue to their left, and between the beach and the highway snaked the railway tracks they'd travelled not even an hour ago.

Nate glanced at Lou. She was staring out the window, maybe at the tracks, her expression stiff, her lips pressed tightly together.

Her hair was a mess, big chunks of it falling loose of what had been a neat braid. On her neck was a red mark, maybe five centimetres long. At a glance, it could be mistaken for something else – maybe a mosquito bite. Or a hickey, even.

It had to say something about him that even now – even after what was definitely the biggest clusterfuck of his career – he could make space in his brain for imagining kissing her neck like that – branding her in that way.

But it was fleeting. He forced it to be.

Because that mark was the burn from a bullet. A bullet that had been so close to killing Lou.

And maybe he could tell himself that he couldn't have prevented that. That it hadn't been his fault. Maybe he could even claim he'd saved her. That by tackling Carey when he had, he'd done enough to misdirect that bullet. But he didn't believe any of it. She should never have been in that position. He should've done better. Earlier maybe, when he'd failed in his attempts to negotiate. Or when he'd failed to take the opportunity to disarm him.

He knew he'd failed her.

And he'd failed Fiona too. It had been seconds between Carey hitting the ground and his ex-wife leaping on top of him, but those seconds should never have existed.

He'd had no right to pause, despite the proximity of the rest of the E-SWAT team. *He* should've been on top of Carey, securing him until Fridge and Smithy had boarded the train.

But he had paused.

To look at Lou.

"He was a *Notechi*," Oscar said. "E-SWAT covert ops took a while to confirm it for us."

"No-ta-kai?" Lou asked, her tone totally normal. As if

she hadn't almost died. As if she hasn't just watched a man die.

"It's Latin," Oscar explained. "Tiger Snakes."

Notechis being a genus of large venomous snakes native to Australia. The Notechi – who had butchered the pronunciation as predictably outlaw motorcycle gangs don't give a shit about science or Latin – were a relatively new organisation. They'd splintered off from the Bald Eagles gang not even six months ago, so it was unsurprising Lou had no idea who they were.

"Bikie gang," Nate elaborated for Lou. "They're expanding their ice business."

"More rapidly than we thought," Oscar said. "Carey was a strong man for them. He's been busy recently. Our intel was that he's been sending a few messages to debtors, and after his arrest, he bashed one of the Notechi small fry to death. He thought the guy had leaked something to the cops, although he hadn't of course. Dumb luck the street patrol caught him, nothing more."

"And this guy was on *bail*?" Lou asked, as Nate was thinking the exact same question.

Oscar shrugged, his eyes on the road. "Our guy on the inside didn't know about the death until the hostage situation was all over the news today. We didn't even know he *was* a Notechi until someone talked and our guy let us know."

And then Carey had shot at Lou, the bullet had jammed some critical part of the door mechanism and kept *all* the doors locked in those critical seconds Nate had fucked up, and Carey had almost sliced his ex's throat open.

Nate looked at Lou again. The view beyond her was now of scrub, and not the ocean, as Stirling Highway wound its way from North Fremantle and into Mosman Park. As if sensing his gaze, she turned from her window to face him. She didn't say anything, and he could read nothing in her expression. She kept her attention trained somewhere on his ruined shirt and didn't meet his eyes.

She'd been like this at the train station: silent and distant. Was she in shock? Was she angry with him?

She should probably be both.

Nate hadn't realised he'd moved his hand across the leather fabric of the seats until Lou snatched her own hand up and lay it in her lap, turning her body as she again looked out the window.

What had he planned to do? Hold her hand?

As if she'd want comfort from him – the man who'd deliberately broken her heart all those years ago and who today had almost got her killed?

Yep. Unlikely.

Inside the SUV remained silent all the way to HQ.

At HQ, no one said much as they made their way to the briefing room. There, the tables were all joined up in a large U-shape, every operator involved in today's hostage situation in attendance, and the large screen at the open end of the U displaying a man with too long hair, a week-old beard, a shit load of tatts – and a not unfamiliar face. It was Damon Nyhuis, one of the guys

Nate went through E-SWAT selection training with more than five years earlier and who was, it would appear, in deep cover with the Notechi. Who knew what name he was using now, or where he was currently located – but he definitely wouldn't *ever* be anywhere near Elite SWAT HQs until his undercover assignment was over.

Sergeant Peters strode into the room shortly after Lou and Nate took their seats at the bottom end of the U.

"Right," he said, in his standard pissed-off-with-the-world tone, "you two going to let us all know what the fuck happened today?"

CHAPTER EIGHT

THE BRIEFING HAD BEEN BRUTAL. SEVERAL HOURS re-living those twenty-odd minutes on that train, with every choice, every decision she and Nate and the team had made, picked at like a scab.

And this was only the beginning. There'd be a hell of a lot more of this: more analysis, more questions, more self-reflection, all with the aim of refining the well-oiled machine that Elite SWAT was. What could they learn from this? How could their procedures be refined? Who needed more training?

It hadn't been about laying blame today. It had been about facts.

And the facts were that not one person at that table considered Lou part of the team. Lou was a witness in their eyes, nothing more, nothing less.

That shouldn't have surprised her. She was on desk

duties. She'd been an *actor* in the surveillance exercise that now felt a million years ago.

Yet, it still stung. Maybe it would've been just the same if she'd just randomly been on the train – if this had all happened a month ago, before her career had been flushed down the toilet. Maybe E-SWAT would've still kept her at a distance. She was a standard-issue cop after all, and they were the elite.

Maybe.

But it was impossible for Lou not to colour everything that happened now with the stain of her error that had landed her at Elite SWAT, and nothing she told herself changed that.

After the briefing she went back to her desk. It was in the same room as the other non-uniform staff at E-SWAT – the receptionist, IT Support, a couple of physical trainers. The desks for the tactical operators were across the hall, and other E-SWAT teams were spread across the four levels of the building.

It was late, well after six o'clock, and her office was empty. Lou dropped down into her seat, the crappy old chair barely moving on its ancient, sticky wheels. She logged into her equally archaic desktop computer and checked her email without really paying attention. She left the emails encouraging her to take advantage of the WA Police's counselling services unread. She'd read them before, after all.

Her lovely new office clothes were in a cloth shopping bag under her desk, and after briefly considering

going home in the borrowed outfit she still wore: deco-
rated with blood from Nate she hoped and not Carey, she
dismissed the idea. Suddenly, remaining in these clothes
that reminded her of yet another professional failure was
impossible, and she headed for the showers.

Being clean made absolutely no difference to her
mood, and neither did re-applying her make-up.

Lou questioned why she was bothering, as she held
the mascara wand somewhere in the vicinity of her
eyelashes. She just stared at herself, at her face neatly
covered in the same brand of tinted moisturiser she'd
worn each day since she was nineteen, and her long dark
hair now neatly pulled back into a damp bun.

But she didn't bother lying to herself. She was
putting on her make-up in case she bumped into Nate. A
man who had probably already left to go home, and more
importantly, had probably already gone home *to his wife*.

Yet here she was.

She put on her mascara anyway.

Stuff it.

She might be a professional failure who inexplicably
harboured feelings for a man who'd dumped her more
than ten years ago, but she was walking out of this Elite
SWAT building looking damn good.

So, she straightened her shoulders, and headed back
to her desk to grab her handbag.

But came to a halt just inside the door to her office.
Nate stood, one hand resting on her L-shaped desk,
waiting for her.

"What do you want?" she said, not giving a stuff about how rude that sounded, then stalked over to her desk, keeping her gaze on her bag and not on him.

Although it was impossible to ignore how good he looked in jeans and a black T-shirt that showed off the power of his shoulders and arms to perfection.

"Are you okay?" Nate asked, as Lou hoisted her bag over her shoulder.

"Sure," she said, and turned to go.

Nate's touch at her arm made her go still.

She looked down at his tanned fingers against her bare skin. His left hand.

No ring.

"Where's your wedding ring?" Lou asked before she had a chance to think her question through.

"Wedding ring?"

Lou looked up to meet his gaze. "You know," she said, deciding to brazen it out. "the ring customarily worn as a symbol of your unending love for your spouse?"

Nate's expression shifted from confusion to ... speculation?

"I don't have a spouse," he said, firmly. "I was wearing a ring today as it activates the microphone on the concealed comms system I was wearing."

"Oh," Lou said. It seemed absolutely the only thing she could say.

Her gaze dropped down again, landing on the small logo printed on Nate's T-shirt, the word scrawled across the hard shape of his pectoral muscle.

No. Not the best place to look.

Her gaze dropped further. To the front of his jeans.

No. Worse place.

"Thank you," she blurted out, knowing she should've led with this. Not only just now but hours ago.

"For what?" Nate said, and Lou was so surprised her gaze shot back to meet with his.

"For jumping on Carey when he shot at me," Lou said. "You probably saved my life."

But Nate shook his head. "No," he said. "I almost got you killed, I—"

"Bullshit."

The voice came from the hallway, and both she and Nate turned towards it.

It was Oscar Shepherd, Nate's sergeant. Not as tall as Nate, but close, with hair clipped so short he was almost bald and the kind of rough-hewn, handsome face that totally pulled that look off.

"It's not bullshit, Macca, I—"

"Bullshit," Oscar repeated. "Honestly, if you could bottle the mope that you two have going on you'd keep a high school going for years." He paused, and looked to Lou, then Nate and back again. "We're going for a drink," he said. "Let's go."

THERE WAS a bar about a block from HQ that was the usual destination for send-off drinks, Friday night drinks, any-type-of-excuse drinks for anyone who worked at Elite

SWAT. Oscar didn't say a word during the short walk, and Nate found himself spending way too much time thinking about how good Lou had looked in her slim skirt and silky blouse when he'd first seen her framed in her office doorway.

He'd never seen her dressed like this. At the academy she'd been in uniform or PT gear, and when they'd been dating they'd never really had an excuse to dress up. Jeans with heels had been about it – and as much as he'd fucking *loved* how Lou had looked in the low-waisted, skin-tight jeans that had been her thing back then – he was definitely a fan of the high-waisted skirt that hugged her hips and butt, and the way her blouse puffed out and was just sheer enough that he got a *hint* of the straps of her bra.

But as they walked, he kept his gaze focused straight ahead.

What had Lou called him? *Some dick who treated me like shit a decade ago.*

Yeah, that sounded about accurate.

But – she'd thought he was married. And she'd *cared* about that.

Because he wasn't blind. He'd seen her expression shift from defiant, to confused and then to relieved. She'd been standing so close to him, looking pretty much everywhere as she avoided his gaze, and she'd *definitely* been glad he wasn't married. Really glad.

But what did that mean?

Not surprisingly, the *Alibi Bar* was pretty empty,

given it was a Monday, and not even seven o'clock. It was part of an old heritage building, with lots of exposed brick dimly lit by the Edison globes that hung haphazardly from the high ceiling. Oscar took a seat at the vacant bar, and Lou and Nate took a seat either side of him. They ordered drinks, although Nate barely tasted his beer.

"You did well today, you two," Oscar said.

"No—" Nate began, just as Lou said exactly the same.

But Oscar interrupted them both. "We got all the hostages off, alive," Oscar said. "The bad guy was the only casualty. Who knows what would've happened if you two hadn't been on that train?"

"I should never have let Carey get that knife to Fiona," Nate said, staring at the bubbles that slowly rose in his beer.

"Correct," Oscar said, in his no-nonsense way. "But you aren't the type of man to make that sort of mistake twice."

Nate flicked his gaze up to meet Oscar's. "No," he said firmly.

"I am, though," Lou said. "The type of woman, I mean."

Nate rested his forearm on the bar so he could see Lou more clearly past Oscar. "What does that mean?"

She rolled her eyes. "It's how I ended up at E-SWAT, Nate. I choked when it mattered, simple as that."

"What—" Nate began, but Oscar interrupted again.

"If you'd been wired up to our comms, Brayshaw, I

would've told you to step aside. Fridge and Smithy are trained for that type of shot, and their firearms are more accurate."

"But if they hadn't been there, Fiona would've been dead." She stared at the short glass of gin and tonic in her hand. "Because of me."

"And if I'd done my job properly, she would never have been in danger," Nate added.

Oscar groaned, and then buried his head in his hands. "Jesus Christ, guys, I get it. We all get it. You aren't perfect. You made mistakes. But you should both know that life isn't like the movies. No one is perfect. *Elite SWAT* isn't perfect. We make mistakes. But we're a team, and the team succeeded today. And you were both part of that team. Okay?" He shoved his bar stool back and stood, then downed the last of his bourbon. "I'm heading home. You two need to talk or decompress or something, and if you're still both self-flagellating tomorrow; sign up for some of the psych services. They're good."

With that he was gone.

Leaving Nate and Lou alone.

CHAPTER NINE

Oscar hadn't even left the bar before Nate had slid from his bar stool to the one his sergeant had just left unoccupied.

Lou looked up at Nate, who now sat really close to her. Oscar hadn't seemed so close, even though she was certain Nate hadn't slid the stool closer. But wasn't that just the thing about Nate? When he was in her vicinity he seemed to just consume space. Consume *air*, even. Consume *her*, really. If she was honest.

That had always been the problem, hadn't it? He had always done this to her.

It had seemed romantic back then. Now, it just pissed her off.

She was an *adult* now. Not some starry-eyed girl.

"Can we talk?" Nate asked. "I think it would help."

Just as when he'd asked at Fremantle station, and

even when Oscar had suggested it, her immediate instinct was to refuse.

As if not discussing what happened would negate it.

She wished. So, in the spirit of now being an adult, she nodded.

And also, in the spirit of being an adult, she met Nate's gaze.

"I'm sorry," she said. "For not thanking you straight away for what you did. I was too caught up in – what did Oscar call it? Self-flagellation? – to do the obvious thing. The stupidly obvious thing." Lou swallowed. "Thank you for saving my life, Nate."

Nate held her gaze. "I would've done the same for anybody."

He was being factual, so his words didn't sting. "I know," she said. "But today you saved *my* life, so *I'm* thanking you."

He nodded. He'd had longer hair when they'd be dating – the type that would flop forward onto his forehead and that he'd rake backwards with his fingers absent-mindedly all the time. More than once, her own fingers had tangled in that hair.

His hair was nothing like that now, being buzz cut short.

I wonder how it feels?

No, she reminded herself. *She would not wonder about that.*

Nate's gaze was impossible to read in the moody

lighting of the bar, but his forehead was creased in thought.

Suddenly, his hand reached out, and his fingers brushed against her neck – just below where the bullet had burnt its path.

Lou went absolutely still at his touch, forcing herself not to lean into his fingers before remembering to lean away.

"Don't," she said.

His hand fell away, but he still leaned close, his gaze still inspecting the mark on her skin. Then his gaze flicked up, to mesh with hers.

Moody lighting be damned, she saw too much in that look: too much of the past.

Tonight, she didn't want to deal with all those messy emotions. She'd had enough to deal with today without Nate doing something stupid like talking about what they'd once had together.

"Lou—" he began.

"I didn't shoot," Lou said, cutting him off. "That's what happened to get me to E-SWAT. I was at a domestic, this guy had just stabbed his wife, and then he came at me and my partner with a knife. Just kept coming." Lou took a sip of her drink, but there was only ice left now. "He slashed at my partner, and got him too, there was so much blood. The suspect wouldn't drop his weapon, he wouldn't back away." Lou swallowed. "He just kept coming at me, and coming at me, until he had me backed up against a wall, and I *still* didn't shoot. I couldn't do it. I choked."

Nate was still too close, but now she liked how close he was. She didn't allow herself to analyse why that was. "What happened?"

"My partner was yelling at me to shoot, but I did nothing. I couldn't do it, I couldn't squeeze the trigger. Not with ..."

Lou put her glass carefully onto its coaster on the timber bar as her words faded away.

"Not with what, Lou?" Nate asked.

"Not with his kids there," Lou said. "There were two of them, two little girls. They were hiding behind the couch, but I could hear them yelling at their dad to stop."

"Did he hurt you?"

Lou shook her head. "No. Backup arrived and they were able to taser him. His wife was okay, by the way, after surgery. So was my partner."

"So, a good outcome," Nate said.

Lou's jerked her gaze up from her empty glass to stare at Nate. "Except I couldn't do my job. Who would the guy had gone after, after me? His kids? Finishing off my partner? There was a guy in front of me who had ticked every box for using lethal force and I hesitated."

"You would've just let him stab you?" Nate asked.

"I guess." Lou frowned, trying to imagine that playing out. "No. I mean, I don't know. Maybe I would've finally gotten the guts to pull the trigger when I saw my life flash before my eyes or something. But it doesn't matter, I was in that house to protect those innocent girls, and by waiting, I put them at risk and my own life at risk. It was stupid."

To Lou's shock Nate nodded slowly. "It was pretty stupid," Nate agreed. "Men who stab their wives and terrify their children – and then threaten *you* with a knife? They deserve what's coming at them. Sounds like your senior sergeant was right, you do need more firearm training, you need to train enough so that if this type of thing happens again, the right thing to do is instinctive."

"Really?" she said, with a huff of surprise. "You're not going to try and make me feel better?"

He raised an eyebrow. He'd shifted slightly and so now the light from the naked globes illuminated the dark bruise on his cheek bone. "You want me to make you feel better about your mistake?"

"No," she said immediately. "I want it to burn."

"I know," Nate said. "I want today to burn, too. Fuck what Oscar thinks."

She gave a surprised laugh. "I think he just wants us to focus on the stuff that went well, as well as what we stuffed up. Like; you disarmed a murderous gunman, and you saved my life."

"And you kept a dozen schoolgirls safe, and probably saved Fiona's life by noticing her in the first place."

His words were pointed, and Lou blinked.

Maybe she needed to take her own advice. "Fine," she said, "I'll take that. But I still didn't shoot when it mattered."

Nate shrugged. "You haven't done your firearms retraining yet, right? I can take you up to the range if you want some extra practise."

The casual words hung awkwardly between them.

Lou pushed her chair back, and slid off the seat onto her heels. "I'd better go," she said.

Nate's fingers snagged around her wrist. "Why?"

He hadn't moved from his own stool. He just sat there, as casual as his invitation to take her shooting.

Seated like this, his gaze was closer to her eye level. She didn't need to look up to meet his gaze.

"Because that's bullshit, Nate," she said. "We're not just going to start hanging out together."

His thumb slid against the veins and thin skin just below her palm. "Why not?" he asked. "We're colleagues, and I'm still a qualified firearms trainer."

Just as he'd been all those years ago, when she'd met him that first day on the range as a cadet.

She looked down at their hands and said nothing.

He followed her gaze, and only them seemed to realise what he was doing with his thumb. That slow, electric slide of his skin against hers.

His touch fell away, and she *hated* herself for being disappointed.

"We're not just colleagues, Nate," she said with more force than she'd intended, her brain unhelpfully sending her vivid memories of waking up in bed beside the man in front of her, those same fingers skimming along the curve of her spine. She shook her head as if to shake those memories away. "We dated. We've seen each other naked, Nate, and I'm sorry but I can't just forget that."

Shit.

That wasn't even close to what she'd intended to say.

It was true, though. And mortifying.

Which meant she simply needed to leave *The Alibi* as quickly as possible.

She didn't look back as she exited the bar with a stiff, awkward stride, and she had absolutely no idea whether Nate had followed her.

She just hugged her arms tight as she silently berated herself for every mistake she'd made – pretty much ever – and kept her gaze on the steps as she navigated the century-old stone paving in her stiletto heels.

Consequently, Lou didn't see who shot at her.

But she certainly heard the sound of the bullet ricocheting off the brick wall behind her. And she certainly felt Nate wrap his strong arms around her waist, and yank her backwards into the darkness of the bar.

CHAPTER TEN

NATE STUDIED LOU AS SHE SAT IN THE FURTHEST corner of *The Alibi,* tucked into the black leather booth, staring at nothing.

Nate had stepped away from the detectives he'd been talking to at the bar, and now he just looked at Lou.

It had been half an hour since the latest arsehole had tried to kill her.

And despite Elite SWAT swarming over the area, the shooter hadn't been located.

But several witnesses had seen a large black and chrome motorcycle charge down the street immediately after the shooting, and while none had recognised the gang colours on the back of the rider's vest, Nate had no doubt that CCTV would confirm what he already knew.

A Notechi had shot at Lou.

And he hadn't been subtle about it.

The Notechi *wanted* it known they'd tried to kill Lou. Or at the very least, known that they'd shot at her.

Why?

Maybe murder hadn't been the aim, as there'd only been a single shot.

But that one bullet had been far too close for comfort.

Not that a bullet anywhere near an innocent person was ever comfortable.

Especially when that person was Luella Brayshaw.

Nate walked over to her. She'd already waved away literally everyone else who'd approached her, and she'd spoken only the bare minimum when they'd been interviewed earlier.

So, he was surprised when she spoke first.

"Can I borrow your phone?" she said, directing her gaze somewhere over his shoulder.

"Sure." He pulled his phone out of his pocket. But rather than handing it to her, he took a seat in the booth and slid towards her.

Lou glared at him, but he ignored that entirely.

Besides, he didn't crowd her. There was space for a whole other person between them. It was a perfectly acceptable amount of distance between two colleagues.

We've seen each other naked, Nate.

No, he couldn't just forget that either. But that wasn't what he was thinking about now, although he bloody well had when they'd been sitting together at the bar. She'd been sitting there, trying to distract him with her mistakes, and she'd failed at that miserably. She'd been so completely the Lou he remembered: defiant and strong and fragile all at once, that he'd been dragged back into memories he'd thought he'd forgotten. Of laughter and sex and ... and ...

But that didn't matter now.

Now, she looked empty, in a way she hadn't after they'd finally got off that train. Then it had been about adrenalin and – he supposed, self-flagellation – and she'd seemed stunned but not in shock.

Now her gaze was blank, her body appearing bereft of energy.

Nate handed her his phone after he unlocked it.

"Thank you," she said. "My phone is in an evidence bag somewhere."

She immediately typed in a number, then pressed the phone to her ear. "Mum," she began, "It's me. Guess what happened again today?"

Nate looked away as Lou spoke, but he didn't leave the booth.

The bar was a hive of activity – E-SWAT team members, plus standard police – the cops that'd been on duty nearby and responded first, detectives, forensics. The Organised Crime Squad would be here too, for sure – anything involving an outlaw motorcycle gang and they were onto it. Although Elite SWAT worked closely beside them, the E-SWAT team were kind of like Organised Crime's muscle. If there was a raid, it was E-SWAT knocking down the door and clearing each room. It wasn't like TV where detectives run ahead of the tactical operators – it was literally E-SWAT's job to secure a location *before* the detectives came in.

So, Nate recognised a couple of the detectives in the still dimly lit bar, now long cleared of patrons. They wouldn't recognise him though; he was always in a balaclava, helmet and his tactical overalls when they'd met him before.

"Thanks," Lou said, and he turned at her soft voice.

She held his phone out. He made sure his fingers brushed hers when he took it back, partly because he was an arsehole who really liked touching Lou, but mostly because he hated how dead her eyes looked. He wanted a reaction.

He got one. She gasped – for not even a second before she swallowed it and narrowed her eyes.

But he'd seen it. *Good.*

"You okay?" he asked.

She nodded her head but then squeezed her eyes shut and went still. "No," she said. Her eyes popped open and she held his gaze. "I guess third time is the charm with people trying to kill you? Once, twice – I shrug it off, it's part of the job. I care more about what I did wrong than the fact I could've died. But tonight ..." Her gaze dropped down to the table where she was tracing invisible swirls and circles with a fingertip.

"Tonight what, Lou?" he prompted.

She looked up again, and now her gaze wasn't empty. Instead it was full. Full of turbulent emotion.

"Tonight, I'm *scared*, Nate." She shook her head. "I hate it."

It took everything he had not to still her fidgeting hands with his own. To squeeze her palm and tell it would be okay.

"Someone shot at you, Lou," he said. "I—"

"On purpose," she interrupted. "He shot at me *on purpose*. I wasn't some random cop who happened to respond to a domestic violence incident, or who ended up on a train with a madman. Whoever pulled the trigger was shooting at *me*."

"We don't know that for certain, Lou," Nate said. "Maybe—"

Lou rolled her eyes. "Oh, come on, Nate. You reckon it's a coincidence? A Notechi dies on a train at the hands of Elite SWAT, and then a Notechi shoots at someone they think is from E-SWAT who was on that train?"

"You know that's one line of investigation, but it's not the only one."

It was true, but Nate knew he was trying to convince himself more than Lou. He didn't want to think about Lou being the target of an outlaw motorcycle gang. It terrified him.

Lou smiled without humour, and ignored what he said. "You reckon it was those 'exclusive images' from the CCTV at Perth Train Station that gave us away?"

As was customary, neither Lou or Nate's details had been revealed to the media, but one of the local news stations had run still images taken from the CCTV at

Perth Train Station of Nate and Lou boarding the train to accompany their sensationalised 'Undercover cops save lives' narrative. That story had been pulled at Elite SWAT's request almost immediately, but – it would appear – not early enough.

Lou, at least, had been identified. Nate probably too.

"Must be," Nate said, and wanted to do actual physical harm to whichever news producer thought putting their images in the public eye was a good idea. It wasn't general knowledge that Carey had been a Notechi, but even so – E-SWAT had an agreement with the local media, and to disregard it this way was bullshit.

And could've got Lou killed.

"Mum is freaking out," Lou said. "So, I had to be all calm and reassuring, like I always am with my work stuff. But this time I didn't believe it, Nate. *I'm* freaking out." She finally stilled her fingers on the booth's table. "But why would they want to shoot me? I didn't shoot Carey, and that's public knowledge. All they know is that an E-SWAT tactical operator shot him, that's it."

"But they don't know which one." It was Oscar who interrupted, his arms crossed, staring down at them both. "One theory is that you're a proxy, Lou, for Elite SWAT. They wanted us to know it was a Notechi who fired that shot, there was no attempt made to hide it. The rider was wearing a balaclava and the bike had no plates, but the gang colours were plain to see. That's deliberate. And I suspect the shot missing you was deliberate, too."

"So, what was the point of it?" Lou asked.

Nate shook his head. "A warning, a statement, an excuse to shoot at someone? Who knows with these shitheads."

Oscar murmured in agreement. "Yeah. Your guess is as good as the detectives at this stage. But whatever the Notechi logic, it's an aggressive move. It's unusual for an OMCG to go out of their way to draw police attention."

"So, what now?" Lou said. "If it was just a statement or warning or whatever, I should be safe, yes? I can go home?"

Her eyes had lit up, and Nate could see her relief at discarding the fear that he knew had overwhelmed her.

But both Nate and Oscar shook their heads. "No Lou," Nate said, and hated seeing that light in her eyes extinguish. "The detectives have recommended you don't go home, and that you're kept at a secure location. Just in case the guy didn't mean to miss and plans to finish off the job."

Lou dropped her head into her hands. "Seriously?" she said. Her neat hair had become less so, and strands had tugged out of her bun to fall around her cheeks.

"Don't stress, Lou," Nate said, "the E-SWAT Close Personal Protection guys will look after you. You'll be fine."

"So will you," Oscar said, looking at Nate. "If this is about revenge, you're as much in the line of fire as Brayshaw is. You're not going home either. The CPP officers assigned to you both should be arriving soon."

His message delivered, Oscar left them alone in the booth.

For a moment they just stared at each other. Lou's eyes were round, but no longer empty.

It appeared she had something else to focus on now rather than fear for her safety.

"I'm spending the night with you?" she said, clearly aghast.

Nate couldn't help but grin. Sure, he could say the obvious: they'd be in separate rooms.

But Lou would already have assumed that.

That wasn't the point.

Twelve years after Nate had climbed out of Luella Brayshaw's bed and run as fast as he could from the first woman to ever love him – he'd be spending the night with her again.

Somehow, the fact they'd not be in the same bed didn't even feel relevant.

They'd be close enough, and they were in this thing together.

That was what made this feel intimate.

They'd never planned to be on that train together today, but it had happened – and together they'd become a team. Without saying a word, they'd been a team for the entire excruciating journey from Perth to Fremantle. Every look, every touch, every move – they'd been aware of each other. Thinking of each other. Looking out for each other.

And now, with that Notechi's bullet, they were a team again.

Luella Brayshaw and Nate Rivers. Together again.

"Seems like it," Nate said, his grin growing broader.

We've seen each other naked, Nate.

And yeah, that kind of made things feel intimate, too.

THIS WAS A DISASTER.

Lou couldn't say she had a better alternative. She certainly didn't want to go home alone tonight. And she wasn't about to stay with her mum and potentially lure an outlaw motorcycle gang to her mother's doorstep.

But did she *have* to be staying in the adjoining hotel room to Nate? Really??

Logic told her *yes*. As if E-SWAT would deploy two totally separate teams of bodyguards – or CPP officers as they were known – when one would obviously suffice.

She got that. But still.

It sucked.

On the plus side, being annoyed at being paired in this way with Nate distracted her from the fear that hadn't stopped prickling its way along her spine.

Even though she knew how carefully the CPP team had driven them both here – to this small, very expensive hotel just north of Perth, so that she *knew* they hadn't been followed – she couldn't relax. It didn't matter that armed police literally guarded her door and this building, every muscle in her body still felt tense, from her toes to her jaw. She was one big bundle of tension, and despite taking deep breaths and mentally trying to release each tense muscle in her body one by one, she was having zero success. She just lay there, on this huge, lovely, hotel bed and stared at the ceiling. Tensely.

She'd changed into the brand-new knickers, T-shirt, and tracksuit pants that someone had obviously been told to go purchase for her to sleep in. The knickers were too big, the tracksuit pants and T-shirt a touch too small, but they would do.

Honestly, the fact she'd worn ill-fitting clothing for most of today was the least of her worries.

Being shot at twice was a bigger concern.

Lou shoved herself up and off the bed to pace the room.

It had lovely carpet, deep and plush; the type you would never lay in your own house unless you *really* loved vacuuming. If she was allowed to open the curtains she'd have a view over the ocean. The bathroom was all marble and expensive tapware, plus it had an awesome freestanding bath.

It seemed rather a waste for her to be here alone.

That thought dragged her gaze to the door that adjoined her room with its neighbour.

Nate's room.

The door between them was locked – she'd checked – but still.

He was *just there*.

The width of a wall away.

The first time she'd found herself staring at that door, she'd changed into her makeshift pyjamas before she got any silly ideas.

Like, knocking on his door.

And what would happen then?

Nothing, probably. They'd maybe talk a bit more about today. Be professional colleagues.

Or, maybe she would burst into tears on his shoulder and tell him how fucking scary it was to be shot at. How if she held her hand up in front of her face now it would *still* be shaking, and she felt that shaking all the way under her skin and into her veins.

Yeah. *No.*

That wouldn't be happening.

Lou kept on pacing, trying to think about anything but trains, or hostages, vengeful bikies, or bullets. Or Nate. Definitely not about Nate.

Then, there was a knock on the door.

The adjoining door.

"Lou?"

Nate's voice was low and husky.

She went absolutely still. As if she didn't move, she wouldn't need to make a decision about what to do. Answer him? Pretend she was already asleep?

"Lou?" he repeated. A pause, then a sigh. "I know you're awake, I've been listening to you pacing for a while."

Oh.

Lou shoved her hands into the pockets of her tracksuit pants, and rocked onto her heels, then her toes. Heels, then toes.

"That's a weird thing to do," she said, before she even knew she planned to speak.

"Tell me about it," he said, and laughed.

Lou padded across the plush carpet to stand on the other side of the door. He must have opened the door on his side to be able to hear her.

"It's creepy as hell, Nate," she said.

"Yep," he said. "That too."

Lou realised she was grinning.

"Why?" she prompted.

There was a soft thud, just above Lou's height – as if he had rested his forehead against the door.

"I've been thinking about how I'd feel if you'd died," he said.

Lou sucked in a gasp. "Lovely," she said, flat as a pancake.

"No, Lou – I'm serious. I could've lost you today."

Her grin had completely dissolved. "You have to have me before you can lose me, Nate," she pointed out. Then added briskly. "Right. I'll leave you to your self-indulgent concerns, given I'm more concerned about *staying alive* than how you may or may not feel about it."

She stalked over to her bed, and rather violently wrenched back the covers.

"Lou!" Nate said, more loudly now. "Please. Don't go. I ..."

"What, Nate?" she asked, against her better judgment.

"Can I come in?"

Lou stared at the crisp white sheets before her. "No," she said firmly.

"Please," he said. "I'd really like to talk."

She shook her head despite knowing he couldn't see her. "I don't want to talk, Nate," she said. "I'm tired."

And she was. She was tired somewhere deep inside her bones, although she doubted her exhaustion could overcome the tension that still consumed her body.

"How about I just do the talking then?"

"Hmm," Lou said. "A man talking at me. Tempting."

Nate's laugh was rich and achingly familiar.

Familiar enough that she turned without volition, but stopped herself halfway between the bed and the adjoining door.

He cleared his throat. And then there was a long silence, as if he was working out what to say.

"If you let me into your room, you can talk as much as you like, Lou, or not at all," he said, finally. "I don't mind. You can tell me how you're feeling about what happened today. Or not. I don't mind. You can yell everything I deserved yelled at me twelve years ago. Or not. I don't mind." He paused, and Lou realised she'd walked all the way up to the door. She stared at the brass polished handle as he spoke. "You can listen to my apology. Or not. I don't mind."

"Your *apology*?" Lou blurted, suddenly spurred into

action.

Her fingers gripped that brass handle and yanked, but the door didn't move.

She'd just about come to her senses – *why would she want to open that door*, anyway? – when the door swung open. Nate stood there in black tracksuit pants and a grey T-shirt. A key dangled in his fingers, which he held up as if in explanation.

"Wait," Lou said. "I didn't mean to try to open the door." She swallowed. "I don't want to hear some stupid apology just so you can feel better if some Notechi murders me tomorrow, okay?"

Nate's eyes narrowed. "Don't joke about that, Lou."

She held his gaze. "You reckon that was a joke?"

"You're not going to die," he said firmly. As if that would make it true. "Elite SWAT isn't going to let that happen."

Lou dropped her gaze now, and stared at her hands. She'd pressed them flat against her thighs, but it made no difference.

"Your hands are shaking," he said and reached for her.

Not cautiously or waiting for permission. He just reached for her, like it was the most natural thing in the world, and dragged her into his arms.

His big, strong arms wrapped around her, and his hand rested amongst her loose hair as he pressed her cheek against his chest. His heart thumped loud against her ear.

"Shh," he said.

And Lou felt abstractly that she should be annoyed at this: at his presumption that his hug would help her, that his voice would soothe her. *Him.* Nate Rivers. Of all people.

But she couldn't work up the effort to pull away. She couldn't work up the *want* to pull away.

Because his touch felt so good. So solid and unyielding, so warm and understanding.

So, she allowed herself to lean into him. To soften her body against him, and to absorb all that warmth and strength and reassurance.

And slowly, gradually, the shaking stopped.

"I couldn't just stay in my room, Lou," Nate said, lowering his head so he murmured into her hair. "I couldn't just leave you alone after you'd told me you were scared."

"I know it's stupid," Lou said. "I know I'm safe in here."

"It's not stupid," he said. His arms held her closer still. "Not stupid at all."

Now that the shaking had stopped, she became more aware of what she was doing, and that she was practically curled around the man she'd hoped to never see again. Her arms were wrapped around his waist and she was pressed against him: cheek, shoulders, breasts, hips.

Yet she couldn't move just yet. For the first time today – for the first time in weeks – she felt secure. She felt safe. Ever since that night two weeks ago, she'd been off-kilter.

Everything had changed and all she'd become was her failure.

Her mother, her few close girlfriends – no one had been able to make her feel better. None of them had been able to truly understand her fury with herself – and if she was allowed to make a phone call and speak to them now, they wouldn't truly understand what she'd gone through today.

But Nate understood. He'd *been* there.

And not only in the obvious sense of being by her side. She knew from their past that he was like her in so many ways. He understood her drive, her passion to be a truly great cop, her frustration when she never reached her own – even she could acknowledge – unattainable standards.

"I'm glad it was you on that train with me today," she said against his pectoral muscle. His new cotton T-shirt had a small embroidered logo that was scratchy against her cheek. "I mean, I know if I hadn't freaked out and run away, then we never would've been on that train, but ..."

His hand on her back slid up to her shoulder and squeezed. "I know what you mean," he said. "We were a team."

Team.

Lou didn't like that word for some reason. Or maybe how he'd said it, like it was special. She leaned back a little in his arms, to put a slither of space between their bodies. "We aren't a team. We just happened to be on the same train together, and I'm just glad that I was with you."

Lou knew how contradictory that sounded, but she needed to be clear. She and Nate were *not* a team. They were not linked in any way, whatsoever.

"Okay, not a team," Nate said, and she knew he was humouring her, and she would've been more annoyed at that if his arms didn't feel so damn good. He looked down at her, with his navy-blue eyes that had always done things to the butterflies in her stomach – and still did so now – and smiled a half smile. "But we used to be a pretty good team though. A long time ago."

Lou had to wiggle away from him now, and she did.

She scrambled a few steps away and crossed her arms as she glared at him. "*You* didn't seem to think so when you snuck out of my bed in the middle of the night and *never spoke to me again.*"

Lou shook her head angrily. She did not want to be having this conversation. Not tonight, not ever.

Nate stepped towards her. He'd been standing in the doorway this whole time, never fully in her room. But now he was, it felt somehow shocking. To have Nate in her bedroom again, after all these years.

"That was a mistake," he said firmly. "I'm so sorry, Lou."

Lou just shook her head in disbelief. "No. I am not accepting your apology so you can feel good about yourself after the Notechi knock me off."

"*Still not funny*," Nate said from between gritted

teeth.

"*What you did is still not okay*," Lou said, mimicking his tone.

"I know," Nate said. "It'll never be okay."

"Uh-huh," she agreed. "Can you go now?"

This was just an awful end to an awful, awful day.

"I meant what I said on the train," Nate said, quickly, as if he needed the words out fast before Lou yelled at him to leave. "You didn't do anything wrong. You didn't do a thing wrong when we were dating."

"Of course I did," Lou said, and shrugged. "We used to bicker about all sorts of silly stuff. We'd argue, or over-react, or misunderstand each other. It wasn't always *totally* your fault." She attempted a breezy smile and failed.

"No," he said, "I think you know what I mean. You were perfect in the way you were with me, you know, open and honest and you jumped all in. I didn't know how to handle it."

Lou shrugged again, determined to be blasé. "You just weren't into me that way, Nate, okay? No need to rehash it. It wasn't a high point of my life. I told you I was in love with you, you weren't in love with me – and while that is okay, running away was not. We had six months together, Nate. I think I deserved to be told you were ending the relationship, rather than eventually working it out myself."

Part of Lou really wanted to ask him all the questions she'd had back then.

Why?

Why had the man who'd been with her every day for months on end just disappear in a metaphorical puff of smoke? He hadn't replied to one text, he hadn't answered one phone call.

This was before even Facebook – when it was so much easier for someone to disappear. And disappear he had.

"Of course you deserved that, Lou. I'm so sorry. I've regretted what I did to you ever since."

But you still did it.

She needed him to leave her room.

"It was cruel, Nate," she said, instead of telling him to go. She hadn't planned to say that at all, but suddenly words were bubbling up from deep inside her. "You hurt me, and worse, *you changed me*. I gave you the power to hurt me by loving you, and you *fucking used that power, Nate*. You used it, and you didn't care that you crushed the kind of naivety that only a twenty-one-year-old woman can have – the naivety that only exists until some man stomps all over her." She strode back to Nate, and looked him right in the eye from an arms-length away. "And you were that guy, Nate. You stomped all over me, and it hurt, damnit. I'm old enough now to know that nearly every woman has that guy. That guy who made her question love, and if she's worthy of love, if she can trust love – all that messy stuff. But why did that guy have to be *you,* Nate? Why did the guy who—"

Her voice cracked, and her gaze fell to the floor. Her

bare feet gripped at the plush carpet, her toes a freshly painted coral in honour of her first day at Elite SWAT.

"The guy who what, Lou?"

She met his gaze again.

She'd made a tactical error standing so close, because even now, even after all this time, and what he'd done – standing close to Nate Rivers *did things* to her. Tummy butterfly things, tingly things, hot awareness between her thighs things.

Things she *did not want.*

But her hormones or something were reminding her of the Nate she'd fallen in love with, the Nate who'd comforted her tonight, the Nate who'd saved her life.

"*No,*" she said to Nate and to herself. "You don't get to ask me questions. You don't get to apologise to soothe your fucking conscience. You don't get *anything from me.*"

"Lou," he said, and oh – his eyes were so blue and so full of stuff she couldn't define: maybe regret, maybe heat. Whatever it was, it was electric, and she couldn't look away. "You don't need to forgive me. You don't need to do anything. But I need you to know I'm so sorry. So very fucking sorry."

And, oh no, his gaze was tracing her face – sliding from her eyes and down her nose, pausing on her lips. No, not really pausing. Stopping. Parking. Staying.

She licked her lips. She hadn't planned it, she didn't want to, or need to – but she did. She licked her lips, and when she saw the heat in Nate's gaze shift to lust – and a lust that so-help-her she still remembered – she licked her lips again.

Oh.

She liked this.

What had she said?

I gave you the power to hurt me by loving you, and you fucking used that power, Nate.

Well, the power she had right now – standing in front of him in tracksuit pants, a pink T-shirt, and no bra – it wasn't about love. But it was power, nonetheless.

It had taken twelve years, and it wasn't the same, or equal. But it was enough.

She took another step closer.

Kissing distance, if Nate just leaned down a little, and she lifted up on her tiptoes.

His eyes widened. "Lou? What are you doing?"

"I want to kiss you," she said.

She said it with no doubt. She was thirty-three years old. She knew when a man wanted her. She definitely knew when Nate wanted her.

"Why?" he said, "I hurt you. You're angry with me. You didn't even like me calling us a team, for god's sake."

"You're seriously going to try and talk me out of it?"

His forehead crinkled. "Lou, did you hit your head today when you fell?" He groaned, his gaze still locked onto her lips. "Oh, fuck, Lou, you have no idea how badly I want to kiss you, but I don't understand what's going on here, I—"

Lou halted his words with her lips.

CHAPTER ELEVEN

OH MY GOD.

She was kissing Nate.

At first, it was just her doing all the kissing. Lou's lips against his, her arms reaching up to wrap behind his neck, her fingers drifting to test the texture of his now short hair.

Verdict: Not as prickly as she'd expected. Smooth. Nice.

Also nice was his mouth, as firm and lovely as she remembered.

And *how* could she remember, after all these years? But she did. She remembered this. She *knew* this, as if kissing Nate had been imprinted into her. Something she could never forget, no matter how hard she tried.

He was holding himself still, his entire body rigid. As in, *his entire body,* and she pressed herself close against the obvious ridge in his tracksuit bottoms, not giving a damn that she'd never in her entire life thrown herself at a man like this, because she knew he wasn't going to push her away.

She knew it as well as she knew his kiss.

And wasn't that just stupid given this was the man who had pushed himself out of her life so brutally all those years ago? The man most likely to push *her* away, you'd expect.

But he wouldn't.

Because in this, in this kiss and whatever she decided followed – *she* had the power.

She absolutely had it, and when she touched her tongue against the seam of his lips – and he opened his mouth just as she knew he would – she revelled in that power.

His body stood motionless, his arms by his sides.

Who knew why he was bothering when she could feel his entire being vibrating with the effort not to move? Was he giving her the chance to change her mind? To come to her senses?

But his lips and tongue had no such concerns.

And the touch of his mouth was *everything*. Hot and familiar and different, and oh so delicious. She could kiss him forever. Make up for twelve years of kisses that were now clearly inferior to what she'd had with Nate, because kissing other men had never been like this, even if until right this minute she'd refused to acknowledge it.

Although – even now it bothered her.

She broke the kiss – but only just. Her breath still mingled with his as she took deep breaths, trying to work out how she wanted to deal with this realisation.

No man had been like Nate. No man had been like this.

Not that she'd dated hundreds of men, but there'd been some. And with them, it had never felt like this. Never felt so electric, so overwhelming so ... almost inevitable.

"Lou?" Nate asked. "Are you okay?"

She met his gaze. This close his eyes were something else, and also so familiar.

The gaze of a man who had crushed her heart.

And if she wasn't careful ...

No.

Stop.

This wasn't about Nate's power, it was about hers.

She let her body sway forward, deliberately rubbing herself against his hardness, loving how it felt against her belly.

See that? She reminded herself. *You* did that.

And *god*, she needed to feel powerful after today. After these past few weeks. She needed to feel powerful and strong and in control after too long finding herself weak and reactive.

Also, she needed to feel Nate.

All of Nate.

She pushed herself up onto her tiptoes and pressed her lips against his mouth again, but only for a moment. This was just a quick kiss, and just because she wanted to and it felt like too long since she'd last kissed him, even though it couldn't have been more than a minute.

Now she spoke against his lips, her mouth brushing against his with every word as she rubbed her belly against the heavy weight of his cock.

"Doing this with you *makes* me feel okay," she said, with absolute honesty. "But please Nate, I *need* you to touch me." She smiled against his lips. "Now, please."

And he did.

Oh, *how* he did, his hands landing in unison on her hips and then sliding up to explore the shape of her waist and then down to curve around her backside.

This didn't surprise her as he gripped her arse and yanked her against him, she hadn't forgotten how much he loved her butt.

Then ... he initiated a kiss. No more letting her lead. No more giving her a chance to change a mind that was never changing.

And his kiss was just as determined as hers had been, as he rediscovered her lips, and tongue, and teeth.

Suddenly, touching his hair was clearly insufficient, and her hands slid down his shoulders – bigger than they'd been at twenty-two – and then her nails dug down the furrow of his spine before slipping up the hem of his T-shirt.

He followed her lead without hesitation, one hand

going straight to her breasts, palming them, then rubbing his thumb over her nipple as he swallowed her sighs and gasps.

Lou tugged at his T-shirt uselessly, too focused on his kiss and his hands on her body to be capable of removing his clothing. Nate was more effective, in a move she had no idea how he managed, her T-shirt was over her head with barely a breath between kisses.

His hands were huge and hot against her back, making her feel small and delicate – but not fragile. Nope, everything about this made her feel strong. Strong and vital and *alive*.

Nate's lips slid their way from her own to trail to her jaw and then against her neck, and to that tickly spot beneath her ear which he clearly had not forgotten.

She practically purred as sensations rioted about her body as he kissed and licked and breathed his hot breath on the skin of her neck, and her body melted in reaction. She rubbed herself against him, her nipples hard against a T-shirt he needed to get rid of.

"Take off your shirt," she said, and made herself step back as he did so, eyeing his powerful biceps and triceps as he yanked the shirt over his head – and she enjoyed that beautiful millisecond where his arms were above his head and her view was completely full of his chest: all tanned skin, and muscles mouth-wateringly defined.

"Jesus Christ," Lou breathed. "Just wow."

"Right back at you," Nate said, his words hoarse, his hands already back on her, one hand sliding under the waist of her tracksuit pants, then her underwear, to grip her bare arse and pull her against him again. So, Lou didn't get to run her hands across his chest the way she wanted, because now she was flush against him, naked breast to naked chest and *hell, yesss*, that was absolutely fine with her.

He took her mouth again as his other hand found its way into her pants, and then he was lifting her off the ground and her legs were around his hips and his strength and urgency, and everything about what they were doing just made her hotter, and wetter.

As Nate discovered for himself when his fingers shoved aside her knickers to touch her *right there*, to slide through her wetness with an appreciative groan and then to circle around her clit in a way that made Lou gasp and jerk against him.

Their kisses were messy and desperate now, each merging into the next, and then Nate was turning her and she was pressed against something – the wall, or the door, she had absolutely no idea but she did voice her disappointment when Nate's clever fingers suddenly disappeared.

"Don't stop—"

But he hadn't at all, of course, and instead those clever fingers placed her on the ground for only as long as it took for them to strip her of her pants and knickers, and then she was absolutely naked – and so she spoke when he immediately went to hoist her up against the wall again.

"Wait," she said, her gaze on the front of his tracksuit, and her brain remembering how she'd so carefully avoided looking at his crotch only hours again and now here she was – allowed to look her fill.

But honestly – all of today just demonstrated exactly how much things could change in a day. In hours. In minutes, in fact.

And so, she reached for him, at first through the dual layers of his fleecy tracksuit and the cotton boxers she knew he still wore because they peeked above the low-slung waist band of his tracksuit pants. But even through those layers he was hot and heavy in her hand, big and thick and *hers*.

Nate had gone absolutely still. They both stood there for infinite seconds, their chests rising and falling as they breathed heavily almost perfectly in sync – as the way Lou had slowed things down not *at all* diminishing how sexy and desperate this felt. How good. How powerful.

His gaze on her as she tracked her fingers up his length and then over to his waistband was all about antic-ipation and need. His, but also hers. Oh, so much hers as well.

At her touch on his belly he sucked in a groan, as if she'd set off sparks at that simplest of contact. His skin was smooth and hot beneath her own, and when she pushed her hand beneath the elastic of his waistband, it was just about the sexiest thing: her hand trapped against him, held in place as she refamiliarized herself with his cock and moved her hand in a way his breathing told her he liked. A lot.

This almost didn't feel real. After all this time, to be touching him so intimately. But at the same time, it couldn't get much more real than this, could it? Standing here naked in front of this man, following exactly what her body wanted to do without overcomplicating it?

So real. So simple. So easy.

"Lou ..." Nate said, his voice deeper than she'd ever heard it. "I'm sorry but I want so badly to be inside you right now, please ..."

Honestly, she had no clear idea what he was apologising for but she definitely knew what he wanted, so she just nodded and before she knew it she was pressed against the door again, her hands gripping at his shoulders and her legs wrapped around him. But when she thought he'd shove down his pants, he didn't – instead he held her still, her hips tilted forward, one hand cupping her backside, the other sliding through her folds, and honing in again on her clit as he looked down between their bodies and at her core.

"You're so wet for me, Lou," he said. He slid one finger inside her, and Lou just about leapt from his arms at how amazing that felt. "So wet," he said sliding in, and out, and in, and out. "I can't believe I'm touching you again, Lou."

No.

Thinking of memories was one thing. Voicing them was not. It felt too ... too ...

Oh, she had no idea, his fingers were doing amazing things and when he slid another finger in she almost exploded *right there*.

But no, that wasn't how she wanted this. This was about power and sex or – oh my *god* she was going to come, and she wanted him inside her because once she came this would be over.

That idea made no sense but then neither did any of this if she thought about it for even a nanosecond. All Lou knew was that she was desperate to come *with* Nate, to feel him inside her right now – to be filled and stretched by him. She *needed* this, she needed him, and she reached for his cock through all the fabric and managed to gasp something unintelligible that clearly Nate got the gist of as then she finally saw his cock and she practically cheered in relief.

"Please, Nate ..." she managed, and then he was there, pushing against her entrance and it felt *so bloody good*.

And then Nate went still. "Condom," he said, pulling away and leaving Lou absolutely bereft.

"I'm on the pill," she said. "And I'm clean, I promise."

He nodded as he breathed hard against her shoulder. "I'm clean too. It's been a while."

Why would he tell her that?

It shouldn't matter. It didn't matter.

But Lou had absolutely no time to work out if it did because then Nate was pushing inside her again and literally how damn good that was, it was *everything*.

She dug her nails into his shoulders as he paused once he was fully inside her, because she couldn't stay still. She wiggled against his hard length, *needing* him to move, needing him to slide in and out of her. Now.

"Nate, please, just fuck me ..."

And he groaned into her ear at the word she knew she'd *never* said to him in bed before but hey – she had learnt a *few* things in the past twelve years – and oh, she liked saying that word to him, liked the power to tell him what to do to her, and loved the power that word had over him in how it plummeted him over the edge of any control he may have had.

Now he was fucking her, and she loved it all: hard and fast and a bit rough and all so, so very good.

Nate's breath was hot at her neck, and then her jaw and then he was kissing her again and it was almost too much – trapped here against the wall and surrounded by so much of the man and what he was doing to her – what they were doing to each other.

He murmured against her lips.

"Touch yourself babe, come on me."

And so, she did, just above where they joined, and it was so wet and hot and *oh my god,* her orgasm hit her like a tidal wave and went on and on, radiating through every inch of her body in a glorious surge of sensation. She wrapped her arms and legs around him harder as she held on tight as he groaned and swore against her ear as he came hard and magnificently inside her.

After, they just stood there for a while.

And for that while, it was perfect.

Nate and Lou, with matching shuddering breathing, basking in the afterglow of something remarkable.

But then, as her breathing returned to normal, everything changed.

CHAPTER TWELVE

One moment, Nate was the fucking king of the world. The next, he was just some dude with his tracksuit pants around his ankles.

And it changed, just like that. One moment Lou was soft and replete and *perfect* in his arms, the next she had slid down his body and then darted away to gather up her clothing which she then held up in front of herself when she turned to face him.

"You should go," she said.

"Why?" he asked, taking his time to pull up his tracksuit pants.

Lou narrowed her eyes. "You know why," she said.

"Nope," he said truthfully. "That was something else, Lou."

He shook his head, unable to fully grasp the words to describe it. Hot, obviously. But also, something more – there was so much of that which he'd remembered – the soft sounds she made when he touched her breasts, the way she unravelled when he slid his fingers inside her, the way she didn't realise how gloriously loud she was when she came.

But there was also so much that had been different. Her confidence in kissing him in the first place. Her assuredness in how she touched him. Her husky, sexy words in his ear.

Just fuck me, please.

Fuck. Just thinking about that made him get hard again.

"Why should you go?" Lou prompted, straightening her shoulders as if she wasn't naked except for the bundle of clothes that barely covered her. "Hmm," she said. "How about, you hurt me. I'm angry with you. And I don't even like you calling us a team."

She was using his words from before.

"Then why did that happen?"

She shrugged. "Why not?"

Then she headed for her ensuite bathroom, not bothering to obscure her rear view.

"So that's it?" he called after her, not understanding what was happening at all.

She didn't even look over her shoulder. "You got to say sorry, Nate, so you got what you wanted. I got what I wanted too. But now you really need to go."

Then she closed the bathroom door behind her, and Nate was left half naked in the middle of the room.

So that was that.

Lou had kissed him, they'd had sex, and according to her – it was that simple.

She'd got what she needed from him.

So maybe it *was* that simple. Her hands had stopped shaking when he'd held her earlier. He knew he'd just made her feel *really* good.

And he *had* got to deliver the apology he'd known was so late to be worthless to Lou – but he'd needed to say it anyway.

Even though, as expected, she hadn't forgiven him. Why would she?

And why, after all these years, would he now care that she did?

So yeah, the sex had been out of this world.

But Nate still walked out of Lou's room feeling empty.

Lou stood frozen in the middle of the opulent bathroom as she waited for the *click* of the door between her room and Nate's closing.

Finally – it did – and she let out the breath she'd been holding.

What had just happened?

She tried to work that out as she had the hottest shower she could handle, as she rubbed herself dry with a white fluffy towel, and then as she brushed her teeth with the tiny toothpaste and foldable brush supplied by the hotel.

Then, as she combed out her hair, she glanced at her reflection in the mirror. Then stopped and *properly* looked.

She was smiling. Like, a proper, satisfied, smug, *guess what I just did* smile.

She shook her head – maybe to shift the smile? And that idea was so ludicrous that a giggle burst out of her throat.

Then a laugh.

After today, of all days, she was laughing.

After a day packed full of self-doubt and self-recrimination – and topped off with fear – she was laughing.

If having sex with Nate could do that, if it could genuinely shift the fear that had so consumed her and replace it with memories of being shoved up against the wall until she came, well ... it couldn't be a mistake, could it?

She'd sent him out of her room in a whirl of fury at herself for what they'd just done, fury at herself for opening herself up to being hurt by Nate again.

But she hadn't done that. Not at all.

Because it was a one-off thing, of course. Never, ever to be repeated.

She was in control here.

As long as it never happened again.

Lou was woken from a dreamless sleep by the jarring beeping of the hotel's clock radio. Then, for the first time in years, she didn't check her phone as soon as she awoke – given it was in an evidence bag somewhere and all. Without her phone to distract her, she was dressed in the same pencil skirt and blouse from yesterday in no time – although her clothes had now well and truly lost their shiny new clothes appeal.

Nate knocked on their adjoining door as she did her hair, but Lou didn't respond – and he didn't knock again.

The knock on her hotel door of the CPP officer Lou did pay attention to, and soon she was in a briefing in a third hotel room, a larger suite with a dining table and enough chairs for Oscar and a selection of other E-SWAT team members that Lou was introduced to in a flurry of surnames.

And, of course, Nate was there too.

He sat down in the seat directly beside Lou's – which made sense, given it was Nate and herself being briefed.

But still, it wasn't ideal. She was close enough to identify the familiar scent of the hotel's soap on his skin, and the entire right-hand side of her body prickled at his proximity. And being that close triggered memories of being even closer to the man beside her. So, so much closer ...

"We recently received some intel from our guy inside with the Notechi." A tall, willowy woman spoke – Senior Sergeant Cripps, from the Covert Operations Elite SWAT team – and her brisk tone snapped Lou's attention back to the far more appropriate present. "It wasn't safe for him to contact us until early this morning, but he's confirmed the detective's assumptions. The shot last night was intended as a show of strength. They're not happy we shot one of their men, and they want us – and the other OMCGs – to know they are armed and prepared to retaliate." Cripps tucked her long black hair behind her ears and curved her lips into a subtle smile. "However, they also don't want the scrutiny of a murder investigation. Our guy is confident that Brayshaw, or Rivers, won't be targeted again."

"Confident?" Nate asked, leaning back in his chair and crossing his arms across his broad chest, an absolute picture of scepticism.

"Very confident," Cripps confirmed. "And this agent is very, very good at his job, Rivers. He knows the outcome of his advice."

"Which is no more bodyguards, right?" Lou asked. She sensed Nate's tension beside her.

"That's correct," Oscar interjected. "With no further threat, we can reassign the CPP team."

It all sounds so sensible. A simple reallocation of resources – which it was.

But those resources had kept her safe.

"What if he's wrong?" Nate asked, voicing what Lou was thinking as he leaned forward in his chair. "What if this guy has no bloody idea at all, and you take his advice, and Lou ends up dead next time?"

Cripps was clearly unimpressed. "I trust my team," she said firmly.

"But he didn't warn us about the shooting, did he?"

Nate continued, no longer hiding the bite in his tone. "Fat lot of good he did for Lou then."

"*Nate—*" Lou began.

"Last time I checked, being clairvoyant wasn't on the undercover agent selection criteria, *Rivers*," Cripps said sharply. "You may remember our agent was involved in the briefing yesterday. When he returned to Notechi headquarters, he worked all night to get the intel we've received, with your safety his highest priority. I trust him. My recommendation is that you trust him too."

Nate's nod was tight, as was his jaw.

"We trust him," Oscar said.

Lou didn't really hear much else of what was said after that. But five minutes later, she was out in the hallway again, with Nate and Oscar.

"Get your stuff," Oscar said, before turning on his heel. "Be at the hotel carpark in five, a car will take you back to HQ."

Then he was gone.

Just like it had been at the bar, Nate stood no closer to Lou in the hallway than Oscar had, yet Lou was just so *aware* of him. She'd never consciously thought last night might have scratched some Nate River's itch and now he'd no longer have this impact on her. But still, it annoyed her that clearly wasn't the case. She wanted to be in control of how she felt around him, and her body kept betraying her.

"I don't like this," Nate said.

Neither did Lou, but instead of agreeing with him,

she shrugged in an attempt at nonchalance. "Doesn't really matter if you do or not, Nate."

She walked the short distance to her hotel room door. Nate followed, but he didn't stop at his door, instead taking the few steps to join her outside hers.

"You're okay with it?" he pressed. "No bodyguards. Everything back to normal. You sure?"

Lou nodded, her gaze on her hands as she slid the room key into the lock and then swung upon her door. "Mmm-hmm," she said, which sounded kind of like she was agreeing.

Her head *wanted* her to agree – the logical part that told her Elite SWAT didn't make these decisions lightly, and if they believed her safe, then she was.

But the rest of her just couldn't. All the tension Nate had helped her eradicate last night was back, tying her stomach up in knots.

Someone shot at me last night, and no one really knows for certain if they're going to do it again.

Although at least her hands were steady on the door as she turned to face Nate, still standing, watching her, in the hotel hallway. If her hands had been shaking, she knew Nate wouldn't have walked away.

How did she know that?

She didn't. Of *course,* she didn't.

And it was dangerous to start thinking she might know anything about Nate at all.

Her gaze flicked upwards to meet his. "We need to hurry or Oscar is going to get cranky."

Nate opened and closed his mouth a few times, as if he had something to say, but couldn't decide if he should say it.

But she didn't prompt him. Continuing a conversation about the fact he *clearly* thought she was still in danger wasn't going to help her head convince her roiling stomach all was well.

And also, last night's apology, and today's concern, it kind of pissed her off. Both the fact he suddenly gave a shit about how she was feeling, but also – mostly – her reaction to this belated consideration.

It felt good to have him worry about her. Even as she'd refused his apology last night, it'd felt good he'd cared enough to articulate it.

"Just don't worry about me, Nate." Lou said firmly.

He shoved his hands into the back pockets of his jeans, clearly frustrated. "How can I *not*, Lou? You walked away from me last night, and next minute you're way too close to a bullet, I—"

"No," Lou interrupted. "You're misunderstanding. I'm not telling you I can look after myself, or anything like that. I'm telling you that you don't get to worry about me. I don't *want* you to worry about me, or pretend to worry about me, or whatever it is you're doing. Okay?"

Lou stepped into the hotel room fully, and let the door swing shut.

Nate blocked it with his hand before it closed all the way.

"What the hell does that mean, Lou?"

She crossed her arms in front of her chest and stared at him. His jaw was tense, his gaze demanding.

"It means, leave me alone," she said simply.

"But last night—"

"Isn't going to happen again," Lou finished. "Life goes back to normal. E-SWAT is a big place, we'll probably rarely see each other." She shrugged, as if last night hadn't been unforgettable. "Yesterday was an intense day, and then last night only happened because of the day we had. It's done, it's over, so let's just move on."

Nate looked like he might say something, so she cut him off the best way she knew.

"You know, kind of how you moved on twelve years ago, right?"

Physically, he didn't react at all. No sharp intake of breath, no change to his expression.

Eventually, he nodded – a sharp, mechanical movement. "Fine," he conceded. "If that's what you want, Luella."

Then he let go of the heavy door, and it swung shut with a final thud.

If that's what you want, Luella.

Lou swallowed strangled hysterical laughter. Of course she didn't want Nate to leave her alone.

If she was honest with herself, she wanted more than anything for Nate to sweep her up in her arms and tell her everything would be okay.

But, he wasn't going to do that. And even if he *did*, a

fat lot of good it would do if the Notechi really wanted to kill her. Or kill Nate, for that matter.

No, last night had been good.

Incredible, her subconscious corrected.

Yes, that too.

It had served its purpose. Maybe it had even been cathartic.

But she knew now why she'd hated last night when Nate had called them a team. She'd hated it because it was how she'd used to think of the two of them, all those years ago. She'd imagined a whole future for them both, together. As a team.

But Nate had never really been into her delusional Nate & Lou team back then, and the team he spoke of now – or implied in his concern for her – was just as fanciful.

She was much better off alone.

CHAPTER THIRTEEN

Years ago, Elite SWAT had transported an old weatherboard cottage to the sprawling rural property in the Perth Hills that the team used for pretty much every type of training you could think of. There was enough space out here for the snipers to practice shooting over kilometres, for the tactical guys to fast rope out of helicopters, and for the bomb squad to blow up whatever they felt like.

Usually, Nate liked coming out here. Especially on a day like today – when the sun was shining, and he wasn't under the scrutiny of assessment. In theory, this was his playground. Here, he got to do all the fun stuff of his job without having to worry about the complications of either real criminals, or innocent civilians.

But today, he just wasn't feeling it.

He stood outside the cottage, in full tactical gear: black overalls, balaclava, body armour, helmet, boots.

The only difference between today and his standard operational attire was that his assault rifle had bright blue splashes all over it because it'd been modded to shoot paint rounds.

(Although, those things still hurt like a bitch if you got in their way).

The cottage was pretty beat up, having had the door battered down an infinite amount of times, and a million flash bangs deployed in its interior. But it served a purpose, and today, Nate's tactical team were using it as refresher training for a mock hostage situation. A few of the guys standing around him were balls of restless energy desperate to get going and to receive Oscar's feedback. Oscar and one of the trainers would observe their progress through the house from a small demountable office nearby that streamed video footage throughout the entire cottage, and the whole team was miked up.

It was a precise, high pressure, exercise, and Nate knew he was *very* good at it. He was team leader today, a role he routinely had on real jobs, and a role he relished.

And the reason he relished the job was because he was so passionate about what he did and so focused on every detail.

But today, he really couldn't give a damn.

Today, all he could think about was Lou.

And not so much the naked version of Lou - although that version certainly got quite a bit of play time – but the Lou who had looked him in the eye this morning and told him to leave her alone.

Clearly, and unambiguously.

She really, truly, wanted him to leave her alone.

And Nate couldn't work out why that shocked him.

Because, objectively, he knew he'd hurt her. He absolutely understood why she'd still be angry. Of *course,* she wouldn't want anything to do with him.

But last night ...

The more he thought about it – and he'd thought about it *a lot* today – the more impossible it seemed it had happened at all. Why, when she wanted nothing to do with him, would she fuck him?

Her excuse that she'd used him for what she'd wanted didn't sit right with him. It hadn't felt like purely a physical exercise. There had been – as there always had been between them – an intensity that was more than just wanting to jump each other's bones.

It had always been like that between them, even that very last night all those years ago. He hadn't left because that'd waned. The night he'd left he still hadn't even got close to having enough of Luella Brayshaw.

Last night only proved nothing had changed in that regard.

So, he still wanted Lou.

And no matter how angry she might still be with him, she didn't hate him enough that she didn't want to touch him. And she definitely didn't hate him touching her.

"You with us today, Rivers?"

Nate blinked, and focused his gaze on the man before him: Cam Westinghouse, or 'Fridge', who'd been on the train yesterday. He was a tall, stocky guy, with sandy blond hair and adorable dimples that everyone at Elite SWAT gave him shit about.

"Yeah, mate," Nate said, pulling himself together. "Of course."

He needed to focus. The other team were out of the house, and he needed to get his team ready.

He needed to do his *job*. Just as yesterday he'd been so fucking focused on Lou he'd almost let Carey kill his ex-wife, today he was letting Lou distract him again.

Distract him from the job that'd been his dream since he'd been a kid.

The same dream job that had pried him from Lou's warm bed twelve years ago.

He held up two fingers as he faced his team. "Two minutes," he called out. *Until go time.*

Each member of his team echoed back: "Two minutes."

Time to get to work.

Today had literally been the most boring day of Lou's career.

Clearly, there was no specific need for her to be at Elite SWAT, so really it was no wonder she'd ended up pretending to be a terrorist yesterday. It seemed highly likely she'd been assigned here purely because they had spare desks. It was literally a place to put her until she requalified to carry her firearm, and so today she'd done a lot of filing, audited the bomb technicians' computer equipment, and put in a new stationary order for the third floor.

There were people employed to complete all those tasks who already worked at Elite SWAT – and they were very nice and willing to find miscellaneous tasks for her to complete – but it all felt very much like being the awkward work experience kid.

So yeah, pretty humiliating for a thirty-three-year-old senior constable.

In her lunch break, she'd gone and bought a new phone, having zero interest in retrieving the phone Carey had used to terrorise his wife and everybody else on that train.

Having her own phone again helped – marginally – to quell the fear that still bubbled if she allowed herself to think about it. After work, as she drove the twenty minutes home in her silver hatchback, she knew if she was suddenly surrounded by a fleet of Notechi on black and chrome motorcycles, she could at least call Nate before they killed her.

No. Call the *police*. Not Nate.

Apart from the not insignificant detail of having deleted his phone number from her contacts *many*, many years ago, Nate was about the last person she would call, ever.

Except he's the first person you thought of ...

Albeit in that very specific scenario.

Given he'd prevented her death at the hands of a man

who turned out to be a Notechi on the train yesterday, maybe it made sense she'd think of him should the Notechi come after her again?

Yeah, right.

Lou gripped the steering wheel so tightly her knuckles turned white.

Nate had returned to her life for less than forty-eight hours and she was already allowing herself to be consumed by him.

As if her mind hadn't drifted to what they'd done last night as she'd filed meaningless papers that should've been archived in 1993. As if it hadn't drifted *a lot*.

So that had pretty much been what had played on loop in her brain today – the amazingness that was having sex with Nate, interspersed with worrying about being murdered on her evening commute home.

Lou pulled into her driveway without incident. She lived in a tiny two-bedroom 1890s worker's cottage on the edge of Fremantle, with a cute postage stamp of a front yard paved with recycled brick and scattered with mismatched pot plants mostly full of succulents or herbs. She loved her house, with its sunny yellow weatherboard walls and white window frames that had been an absolute bastard to paint – but tonight she'd rather it looked a little less adorable and a lot more secure. She didn't even have an alarm system or a security screen protecting her (beautiful) stained-glass panelled door.

She felt mildly ridiculous as she checked over her

house – checking under her bed, and inside every cupboard for lurking Notechis. There were none.

So finally, she changed into jeans, curled up on the couch and called her mother for a chat, and pretended everything was totally fine.

"No, Mum, nothing to worry about. If Elite SWAT think I'm safe, I am."

She certainly didn't tell her mum about the persistent prickling at the back of her neck, or her absolutely certainty that she wasn't going to be sleeping tonight.

But she kept on trying to convince herself everything was totally fine as she ate dinner (leftovers from dinner with her mum on the weekend), and watched the least violent show she could find on Netflix.

But the absolute proof that she wasn't fine, was when a knock on the door almost gave her a heart attack.

Not so much her reaction to the arrival of the unexpected visitor – as telling as that was – but to how she felt when she saw the unexpected visitor was Nate, standing in a pool of light on her teensy verandah.

Because her reaction to seeing the man she'd told to leave her alone was not anger, or even frustration, but instead absolute relief.

But even so, no way was she inviting him in.

"Go away, Nate," she said, only partly opening her front door.

He was wearing black jeans and a slate blue T-shirt, and looked just as gorgeous as usual.

"You don't want to know why I'm here? Maybe I've got something important to tell you."

Lou shrugged. "I'll take the risk."

She closed the door but had only taken a step away when he knocked again.

"I'll do this all night if I have to," he said, his voice barely muffled by a door that had never seemed flimsy until today.

With a sigh – and Lou didn't know if it was aimed at herself or Nate – she opened the door. And stepped outside.

It didn't seem wise to have Nate in her home.

"How did you find out where I live?" she said, keeping the door opened behind her.

Nate barely moved, so she took a step back to put some space between them. Her bare heel brushed against one of the nest of terracotta pots she had arranged beneath her front window, and when she looked down she noticed a small mound of dark potting mix on the jarrah decking, as if someone had knocked over one of her pots and done a poor job at putting it right again.

"Lou?" he asked. "Is something wrong?"

She shook her head. "No," she said. Anyone could've knocked it – a delivery driver, maybe. Or maybe she did.

She met his gaze and narrowed hers. "You didn't answer my question."

"I looked you up on the E-SWAT system," he said, totally unapologetic. "And here I am."

"Why?" she said. "I asked you to leave me alone."

"No," he corrected. "You told me to leave you alone."

For some reason that made her smile despite how bloody annoying he was, and she fought hard so Nate wouldn't notice.

The glint in his eye told her she'd failed.

God this was frustrating.

She swallowed and straightened her shoulders, reminding herself why she'd told him to leave her alone in the first place. *He doesn't get to pretend to care about me.*

"Why are you here, Nate?" she repeated, her words firm.

His gaze was direct, his words as firm as hers. "Because I don't like the idea of you being here alone."

Lou made herself sigh. "If E-SWAT says I'm safe, then—"

"You don't really believe that."

She raised her eyebrows. "You don't trust the most highly skilled police officers in the state?"

"I trust they've weighed up the risk level and assessed it as low," Nate said. "That isn't the same as guaranteeing your safety. You and I both know even the best can make mistakes."

He wasn't trying to be cruel, just make a point, but his words still felt like a punch to her gut. Yes, she knew all about making mistakes.

She hugged herself, rubbing her hands up and down her upper arms, now pebbled with goose pimples in the cooling evening air.

"You can't stay here," Lou said, but without bite.

Had Nate heard that concession?

He shrugged. "No problem." He nodded at the steel grey dual cab ute parked across the road. "I planned to sleep in my car anyway."

Yes, he absolutely knew he'd won.

"No, you didn't," she said. "You planned to tell me that so I'd feel bad, and invite you to sleep on the couch instead."

"Almost," he corrected. "I figured you'd last about an hour before your guilty conscience had you inviting me in – but I'll happily skip that bit. Thanks."

Again, she had to fight against the urge to smile. "You think you know me so well," she teased.

"No," he said, his tone utterly different now. No humour, no smugness. "I don't think that at all. A lot has changed in twelve years."

Lou blinked. "Has it?" she asked, before she could think that one through.

Something hot flared in his gaze – the thing between them that definitely *had not* changed in the past decade: this instant, electric attraction between them.

But as she ignored her own visceral reaction to Nate and pretended her belly wasn't flooded with heat, she reminded herself what hadn't changed.

Nate had hurt her. And she wasn't giving him the chance to do that again.

She forced a laugh, and shook her head, as if bemused by her own question. "I know what's changed," she said. "Me. I was so young, so naïve. To think I thought what we had was love."

She managed another breezy laugh, this one quite convincing.

"It was l—" Nate began, then went abruptly silent.

Lou shook her head again. "No," she said firmly. "While I don't forgive you for what you did, you were probably right to do it. I was infatuated with you, imagining so much that wasn't there. I didn't know what love was."

This was all absolutely rubbish, or a variation of the rubbish she'd told herself over the years.

That maybe she'd imagined the connection between them. That maybe she'd confused lust with love.

Just ways to deal with having her heart broken. Ways to make what had been so huge at the time something she could manage and move on from.

"And you do know what love is now?" Nate asked.

His eyes had revealed so much tonight – his determination to stay here all night, his humour as he'd teased her, the heat of his attraction to her.

But he revealed nothing now.

"Of course," she lied. "I'm a grown-up now. I want more than just puppy love."

Oh, he didn't like that. His eyes narrowed.

"We had more than that," he said.

"No," she said firmly. "We didn't. Clearly."

Or you wouldn't have disappeared.

He knew that too, as he didn't argue any further.

Lou closed her eyes. It was so tempting to just tell him to leave, but she knew there was no point. The furthest he was going away tonight was to the passenger seat of his car.

Earlier today she'd told herself off for thinking she could anticipate Nate's actions, but she did know that for certain. Nate had made his mind up to be with her tonight, to protect her, she supposed.

He wasn't going anywhere.

And that in itself was *more* tempting than the uselessness of pushing him away. The idea of Nate being here for her, *needing* to be here for her, verged close to intoxicating.

Dangerously, it wasn't only because she was genuinely scared of the Notechi. The fact that an outlaw motorcycle gang could be planning her demise had literally not even crossed her mind since Nate had turned up on her doorstep.

Nate did that to her. Distracted her from her own murder.

That made her laugh.

"You okay?" Nate asked, his face an adorable, handsome picture of concern.

Oh, *fuck*. It would still be extremely unwise to let Nate inside.

But still, that's exactly what she did.

CHAPTER FOURTEEN

Lou's house was full of colour. From the green velvet couch, to the framed vintage movie posters, to the glass vases that dotted her bookcase and sideboard – one green, another purple, another pink.

It was … cute. A really cute house.

And it was not at all what Nate had expected.

When they'd been dating, Lou had lived in a share house with a couple of other female recruits. That place had been a mission brown 1970s disaster, its one redeeming quality being how far away Lou's bedroom had been from the other two girls. Her room then had been classic student style – almost exclusively flatpack furniture, and a free-standing clothes rack on wheels housing her entire wardrobe.

Back then, Lou had gone to zero effort to decorate. Her goal had always been to pass her training and as soon as her pay jumped up once she was out of the academy, to get her own place.

"This is a nice house," he said.

Lou had been leading him through the small lounge to the kitchen, and she turned to raise a quizzical eyebrow. "You sound surprised?" Then she read his mind. "Expected circa 2005 Ikea, did you?" She grinned. "I've worked out what I like since then."

She turned and continued onto the kitchen as Nate tried to work out if that last sentence had been as packed full of subtext as it'd sounded.

He rubbed his forehead. *Shit*.

This was messy. Their past, yesterday, *last night*, filled every molecule of air within Lou's house. It was impossible for him to be here without bringing all that complication with him.

He hadn't expected anything less, of course.

It certainly hadn't stopped him from looking her address up in the work system. He could get in a fuck tonne of trouble for that, but he hadn't cared. He still didn't care.

Because after he'd shoved Lou out of his brain long enough for his team to ace the hostage scenario they'd run through today, he'd gone back to remembering last night.

Yes, the best bits, obviously – how hot it had been to have Lou like that against the wall, to have her so eager, so wet for him ...

But also, the rest. How her hands had been shaking. Her fear back at the bar straight after the shooting, the wobble in her words: *Whoever pulled the trigger was shooting at me.*

For all her bravado this morning, he was suddenly certain she wasn't cool with the removal of the CPP team. She wasn't cool about it at all.

But she was letting her own – negative – feelings for him cloud her judgment. She pushed him away this morning because he was a dickhead a decade ago, not because she was supremely confident in the intel provided by an undercover cop she'd never met.

Or at least, that was Nate's theory.

But he'd needed to test it – so he'd driven here, fully prepared to be sleeping in his car all night. He'd even chucked some blankets in the back of the ute.

Because he wasn't capable of leaving Lou alone tonight.

"Have you eaten?" Lou asked. She leaned back against the wooden benchtop, the white cabinets a stark contrast behind the dark brunette of her hair.

He nodded. The brown paper drive-through bags were in the footwell of his car.

"A drink would be good, though?" he asked, and once again Lou raised an eyebrow.

"Shouldn't we have our wits about us?"

She was teasing, and he'd only been after a water – but still he replied seriously.

"I asked around a bit at work, about the source of the intel. I remember him from the academy, and he was a good guy then, and everyone seems to agree he's a great cop now. Keeps to himself, although probably a good trait given his current job."

Lou's lips curved into half a smile.

"But the feedback was consistent – he's trustworthy. Plus, Organised Crime and Covert Ops definitely know what they're doing. They know how these gangs operate, and obviously they endorsed the recommendation to pull the CPP team," he continued.

"So, you don't really think that the Notechi are going to be murdering me tonight," Lou said. She said it in a conversational tone that made Nate narrow his eyes.

"No," he said. "I don't. And I really wish you'd stop joking about dying."

"I wasn't joking," she said, then paused and met his gaze. He was still on the other side of the kitchen, although it was such a small space that it wasn't really all that far away. She'd pulled her long hair into a loose plait that fell down her back, and the soft light thrown by the single pendant light above the counter created long eyelash shadows on her cheeks. "So, you don't really think I'm in danger, yet you're here."

He nodded. "Like I said before, even the best make mistakes."

She looked at him with an assessing gaze. "Do you want a drink then?"

"Yes," he decided. "I do."

Lou didn't have any beer or bourbon, but she did have red wine. They ended up in her lounge room, Lou on the two-seater couch, Nate on the mismatched brown leather armchair which Lou had specified he sit on.

You sit there, she'd said, her expression implying she expected him to devour her if they shared the cosy couch.

Which was probably accurate.

Ten minutes alone with Lou in this cute little house, and it was impossible to not get seduced by the intimacy of it. Or by the intimacy of *her* in casual clothes and her bare feet tucked up under her as she swirled her wine in a stemless glass.

What was the reason they weren't supposed to have sex again?

And what was the reason he ever left her in the first place?

That reminded him to sit where he was told.

"So," Lou said into the awkward silence. "You did make it to Elite SWAT. I remember it was always your dream. Congratulations."

"Thanks," he said, then cleared his throat. He sounded as awkward as the silence had been. "Do you like working out of Coogee station?"

She took a long sip of her wine, her gaze aimed down at the knotted rag rug on her floor. "You know where I work?" she asked.

"Yeah," he said. "I know you went north of the river for a few years, then to Fremantle, then Coogee."

He wasn't sure why he told her all of that.

"You looked that up today or something?" she said.

She was looking at him now, her forehead crinkled into a frown.

"No," he said. "I've uh," he swallowed. He sounded like a stalker, but he found he needed to tell her the truth. "I kept tabs on you, I guess. Asked about you occasionally. How you were going."

He couldn't work out her expression at all. Was she freaked out? Flattered? He had no idea.

"Why the hell would you do that, Nate?" she said, then stood up and walked over to her bookcase with stiff strides.

Right. Not flattered, then.

Her back was to him, and he watched as she took a deep breath. Then another.

"I'd look you up sometimes on Facebook too," he said. *Why was he doing this?* "But you always keep your profile pretty locked down. I like the dress you're wearing in your current profile photo though, the red one. You look hot."

She took another deep breath, still keeping her back to him. Then, as he watched, she drained the rest of her wine, and placed the empty glass beside one of her coloured vases on a shelf.

She didn't say a word, and then Nate found he'd stood up.

For a minute he just stood there, trying to work out what to do now. Tension filled the room, but then as he'd noted before – tension was *everywhere* when he was with

Lou. Right now, the flavour of tension radiating from her was definitely angry, but not just that.

No. That was the thing with them, wasn't it? It was always more. Twelve years ago, and now as well.

She was angry with him, and yet he still felt compelled to go to her. And somehow, he knew, like – deep down *knew* – that part of her wanted him close to her too. Not the logical part of her, sure. But the part of her that kissed him last night. And that let him into her house tonight.

He went to her, his sneakered feet almost silent on the rug. But she knew he was there. She didn't say a word, and kept on studying those books in front of her as if they held all the answers.

"Of course, I looked you up, Lou," Nate said. "And I asked about you. You were ..."

He struggled to work out what he was trying to say, trying to grasp the right word.

She spun around abruptly, so she was right in front of him, her chin up as she glared at him.

"I was the girl you just weren't that into, right, Nate?" she said. "Can we stop going over all of this? I don't want to hear about how you kept tabs on me, like I was some sort of lovesick trophy for you. Did you look me up between girlfriends? When some girl dumped you? To stroke your ego, to remind yourself that hey – this stupid girl is still pining over me?"

"*No*," he said, "of course I didn't, I—"

"But the jokes on you, right, Nate?" she continued.

"Weren't you listening before? I grew up after you left. You treated me like trash and I learnt from that. I realised how stupid I'd been to say that I loved you, when I didn't even know what the word meant yet. I haven't been pining for you. Not at all."

Her gaze was hot and direct. Furious.

The idea of Lou dating other men triggered a wave of jealousy Nate was helpless to tamp down, even knowing how inappropriate it was. Who was he to be jealous of the woman he'd just thrown away ...

"I *never* looked you up, Nate. I didn't know you worked at Elite SWAT because *I didn't care*. I never asked about you, I never thought about you, I never fucking Facebook stalked you. Because you ended what we had and so you being in my life was *done. Forever.*"

She turned on her heel.

"I'll go get some blankets so you can sleep on the couch," she said. "I'm going to bed."

But Nate followed her, grabbing her hand in his.

She went still, then slowly turned to face him.

Inexplicably, she didn't tug her hand away.

And because he couldn't help himself, he ran his thumb over the delicate bones of the back of her hand. Caressing her.

Lou gasped, and her gaze went soft – just for a second. A nanosecond. But he saw it, before she tugged her hand away.

She still wants me.

Oh, and how fucking badly he still wanted her. *Needed* her.

How could he have been so fucking stupid?

"I was young and naïve too," Nate said, his voice rough and raw. "What we had was so intense. The way I needed you was *so intense,* Lou – do you remember?"

She didn't speak, or nod, but he saw the flicker in her gaze.

Yes. She did.

"You were in my thoughts from the moment I woke up. You were everything to me. *I* was infatuated with you, you must have known that. I couldn't get enough of you."

She shrugged, but it was an unconvincing movement. "That was just sex."

"You know it wasn't."

She shook her head, and with that she was clear. "No, I didn't," she said. Her voice was soft. "Nate, I was twenty-one. I was every insecure young female stereotype in the book. I did not know that at all."

Her words were like a punch to his gut. She'd felt like that and yet still had the courage to say she loved him?

He felt sick with what he'd done to her, in a way he hadn't felt back then. He'd been so selfish. So stupid. "I was getting shit from my mates."

Lou's expression was appropriately disgusted at how pathetic that sounded.

"And my dad," he continued. "My dad was *concerned.*

That's exactly how he put it: 'Nathan, I'm concerned about you and this girl'. He said it wasn't normal, that it wasn't healthy. That I was going to put my whole future in jeopardy if I didn't get over this obsession with you."

"Obsession?" Lou repeated, clearly disbelieving. "You were so not obsessed with me."

He had to touch her now, and so he did, circling his hands at her waist and yanking her up against him.

"Oh my god, Lou, how can you think that?" She felt so good against him, her softness against his hardness. Her belly, her breasts, her thighs. "I know you can feel how it is between us, how it still is between us."

Although, even that wasn't accurate. Now, it *was* different. Maybe because they were older, who knew? But what they had now was even more overwhelming than before, that had him listening at her hotel door, or turning up at her doorstep. Just needing to be with her. Close to her.

Lou just stood there, letting him hold her against him.

Her arms hung by her sides, but she had her gaze on him. She wasn't trying to pull away, but she wasn't reciprocating either.

She was just still. Warm. *Hot*. Lou, in his arms.

And it felt so good ... but not enough. Because he needed her hands on his body. He needed her to be as overwhelmed, as obsessed as he felt.

So, he needed to keep on talking.

"I was obsessed with you, and everyone I knew had never seen me like that. I was distracted when I wasn't with you. At work I got pulled aside once. They were worried about me, thought something bad was going on in my personal life. That got back to my dad through his contacts, and he was unimpressed."

Oh, it had been a mistake to grab Lou. Telling her this with her body pressed against him was so revealing. He could feel her body tense and flinch as she reacted to the idiotic decisions of his past.

"I guess I let all that crap percolate in my brain. At first, I told everyone to fuck off, you know? Because I wasn't going to break up with you just on their say-so. Of course, I wasn't. And then—"

"And then I told you I loved you," Lou said. She looked him right in the eye as she said it, exactly as she had all those years ago.

Just like that, he was there again. Twelve years ago, with Lou collapsed naked against his chest, their breathing still coming fast and hard after the fucking miracle that was sex with Lou. And then she'd levered herself up, her hands on his shoulders, her hair tumbling down over her breasts and arms. He remembered thinking how amazing she was. How he'd never seen anything so beautiful in his life.

I love you, Nate, she'd said. She'd said it clearly, and firmly. Like she'd put a lot of thought into it but was now going all in. And of course, it was a big decision for her. A huge decision.

But he hadn't said a word.

He'd kissed her again. Then he'd crawled between

her legs and made her come with his mouth and then she'd fallen asleep and he'd just laid staring at her for hours.

Then, just before dawn, he'd kissed her on her lips as she slept, and said good bye, and sorry, and thought about writing a note but was too gutless to do any of that.

She'd slept through it all, and then he'd been gone.

Gone from her life forever.

But now she was in his arms.

"The way I felt when you told me that ..." Nate said. "It was *huge*. I thought so many things. Panic, and fear, and also how much I liked you – and what did that mean? I was twenty-two and my whole life was ahead of me, and here I was wrapped up in this girl and my whole life had just narrowed down to *you*. And I kind of did know it wasn't healthy, and I was too dumb to think that maybe I could work through that. That I could balance how I felt with you with the rest of my life. Come up for air occasionally but still be with you."

He shook his head, because he was thinking aloud, for the first time really unpacking what had happened all those years ago. Understanding his decisions and not focusing on the relief of his dad and his friends when he'd gone back to being just Nate. Nate who was always available to go out with his mates. Nate whose single-minded obsession was work and not Luella Brayshaw.

"It wasn't until yesterday that I questioned what I did," he said honestly.

Lou shut her eyes at this admission, and took a deep breath.

"You thought you did the right thing," she said. "You'd hurt me but it was for the best, right?"

"I'm so sorry, Lou," he said, and his voice cracked and his throat felt strangled.

"But why do it the way you did?" she said, her gaze locked with his again. "Why without a single word. Without one reply to my text messages, or my phone calls?"

He smiled, because it was so fucking obvious now. "Because if I'd done that, it would've started again. I would've been back the second I heard your voice. The second you let me see you again."

Lou dropped her forehead against his chest, and everything in him was focused on her in his arms. How her waist felt beneath the spread of his fingers, how her breasts felt against the wall of his chest, how he could feel the warmth of her breathing through the thin cotton of his T-shirt.

He didn't move. He barely breathed.

She was thinking something over. He *knew* she was. And it was important.

He just needed to wait. To give her time.

He had no idea what she was thinking – to throw him out? To yell and scream at him the way he deserved?

Or something else? The something else that kept her in his arms. That had allowed her body to settle subtly against him as they'd been talking. Because now she was pressed as close against him as was possible with clothes on. And having her close like this felt more natural, more perfect, than just about anything.

But it could be over at any moment.

As this time, it was Lou's decision to make. Not his.

Because, he knew, utterly and completely that he wasn't walking away from Luella Brayshaw again.

CHAPTER FIFTEEN

WHAT WAS SHE DOING?

Lou breathed in Nate's scent as she stood close against him. He smelled like laundry detergent and the same deodorant he'd worn twelve years ago and just simply like *Nate*. Delicious, and sexy, and overwhelming.

I was obsessed with you.

Oh, those words were so seductive. They could so easily override logic and common sense, and soften the memories of the past.

If she let them.

That was the thing, right?

She was in control here. She absolutely knew it.

Nate was waiting for her. Waiting for her to react to all he'd said. To tell him to go to hell – as she knew she should. Or ... something else.

I was obsessed with you.

See, that wasn't the same as love, for all that Nate had declared they'd had more than sex between them.

He hadn't mentioned love at all.

But then, hadn't she already told him she'd simply been infatuated too? Maybe she *had* been right in how she'd minimised their relationship after he'd left, telling herself it was puppy love, not really love. Whatever.

Maybe she'd just been obsessed too, the way she absolutely was again now.

Because honestly, she was obsessed with Nate. From the second she'd seen him on that train until right this moment. To believe anything else would just be a lie.

That obsession was constantly in the air between them. It was in everything they said, everything they did.

Acting on that would be so easy. So natural. So inevitable.

But at what risk?

Nate's fingers flexed against her waist. His thumbs were just above her hip bones, and she knew he knew how sensitive she was in that little hollow beneath them. If she let him, he could make her feel *so* good. She could make him feel so good, too.

They could feed each other's obsession.

Would that be so bad?

She lifted her head, and Nate's gaze was there waiting for her. She tried to work out what he was thinking, and some of it was obvious.

Regret – and she believed he felt it now. He felt like

absolute shit for what he'd done, and belated or not, he deserved to feel that way.

Also, lust. But that was kind of a default with them, wasn't it?

There was more too, but she suddenly didn't want to, or *couldn't* make herself analyse that. It felt too complicated, too outside this neat new concept that was being simply obsessed.

Being obsessed with Nate and him with her – that put them on equal footing.

No risk. So much reward.

No vulnerability like saying *I love you* all those years ago.

Being obsessed could justify reckless behaviour.

Like pushing herself up onto her toes, and pressing her mouth against his.

He groaned, maybe she did too, it really didn't matter, because they were kissing and it was so, so very good.

Her hands were greedy now, after waiting so patiently by her sides for so long. So now they grabbed at Nate's clothing, shoving up under the fabric of his T-shirt to slide up the furrow of his spine, and to scrape her fingernails lightly and not so lightly against his skin.

His lips were hot against hers, their tongues tangled, and no matter how his mouth slanted against hers it was all amazing. Good, great, like no other kiss she'd experienced. Nate was like nobody else.

His hands were greedy too, cupping her backside

through her jeans, grinding her against his erection in a way that made her gasp and go liquid between her thighs.

At some point she was pressed against the wall but then he was murmuring against her ear, "A bed maybe, this time?"

And she must have nodded or gestured in the vague direction of her bedroom, because suddenly they were there, and Nate had scooped her up and practically thrown her onto her bed, his huge body following closely behind.

He shoved her bra up above her breasts, her T-shirt too, and then his mouth was on her nipples, nipping and kissing and sucking and *oh fuck* it felt remarkable.

She squirmed beneath him, unhappy that his clothes were in the way, although she kind of liked the abrasion of the fabric of his jeans and hers against her core as she rubbed herself against him.

He reared up to yank off her T-shirt, and in that moment, he was lit by only the moonlight that pushed through her closed bedroom blinds and the residue of the hallway light given neither of them had thought to turn on a light in her room.

His body was beautiful, and heavier with muscle than in his twenties, a combination of years of hard work and simply maturity, as at twenty-two he hadn't been the man he was now. Lou pressed a hand against his chest when he would've otherwise laid on top of her again, and his eyes went wide.

"You want to stop?" he asked, with what could only be described as horror in his gaze.

Lou laughed. "No," she said, and then she moved until she was kneeling in front of him on the mattress, and then she reached out and placed her palm flat against his heart.

Nate went still as her other hand joined the first and then slowly she slid her hands down his body, her fingers discovering the curves and undulations of his musculature. His skin was smooth and so, so warm. His body stunning.

"You're the same, but different," Lou murmured.

Nate leaned forward as her fingers reached the waistband of his jeans, his breath hot against her neck, her ear. "You're so beautiful," he said. "I can't believe I was so fucking stupid, Lou, that I—"

She leaned back and pulled her hands away. "*No*, Nate," she said. "Just *don't*, okay?"

She didn't need reminding of his rejection, no matter how prettily he'd justified it, not now when she was about to be naked in his arms.

This was about being reckless, being *obsessed* in the now – not being distracted by the hurt of the past.

And as if to remind herself, she grabbed the edges of the T-shirt that had worked its way back down over her breasts, and tugged it up and over her head, her bra following close behind it.

"Lou ..." Nate breathed, looking his fill just as she had only moments before. This was probably the moment she should feel self-conscious, but she didn't. Not at all. It just all felt so good with Nate, the way he touched her, the way he looked at her.

He reached for her again, his fingers curling into the waistband of her jeans, and then somehow, she was on her back and her jeans were being shimmied away. Then his breath was hot against the satin of her knickers, his fingers sliding just under the edge of the elastic, but no further.

"This okay?" he asked.

"*Yes*," she said. Begged, really. "*Please*,"

Then the satin was gone and his broad shoulders had spread her legs as he settled between them.

"Shit, Lou, I missed this."

And she was way too far gone to tell him off for mentioning the past, and honestly this wasn't really the time as the moment his tongue touched her clit ... *oh fuck* ...

His tongue knew exactly what she liked, how hard, how soft, how everything. As her insides swirled and tightened with sensation, one big hand cupped her arse and the other was – *oh my god, that was new* – at her core and then he slid two fingers inside her wetness just as he sucked hard on her clit. Just like that she was coming hard, her butt coming off the mattress as her heels dug into the sheets.

When the waves of her orgasm had begun to dissipate and she was capable of controlling her limbs, she propped herself up onto her elbows to look down her body at Nate, who still lay between her legs, his breath still fanning her sensitive skin.

It was incredibly hot to have him like that, her legs still akimbo around his shoulders, the sheer size difference between them both juxtaposing his strength and power and her supposed vulnerability in this position.

But she didn't feel vulnerable. At least, not physically. Just like she had in the hotel room last night, she felt powerful with Nate like this. He made her feel powerful, in the way he responded to her, and the way he so obviously took pleasure in the way she responded to him.

On cue, he smiled. A sexy, devastating smile, that had her reaching down to tug at his shoulders and urge him up her body for her kiss. She could taste herself on him, and she luxuriated under his weight as they kissed and kissed, his hands sliding up and down her sides, shaping her waist and hips and butt.

Then she pushed on his chest again. "Onto your back," she said between kisses, and when he was, she traced her way down his sternum and belly with her tongue, then smiled against his skin when he groaned as she reached the button of his jeans.

He helped her tug them off, then his boxers, and then finally she held him in her hands, her fingers encircling his cock as she licked her way around the tip.

But before she could take him into her mouth he was grasping at her shoulders.

"Lou, *fuck* that feels so good but I don't want to come

in your mouth tonight and honey fuck I will if you do that."

So instead she straddled his body, and he kissed her again and again as she reached between them both to guide him where she was hot and wet and so ready for him.

She hissed as she slid herself onto him, loving how he stretched her, amazed at how desperately she'd needed to be filled by him, needed to have him like this: so close, so hot, so *right*.

She sat up on him, her hair loose now having lost its tie who knew when, and it cascaded down her shoulders. She closed her eyes, just giving herself a moment to enjoy this, to *feel* this: how good it felt to have Nate's cock buried deep inside her, how powerful she felt to know how desperately Nate wanted to move – but that he was waiting for her. He was watching her from hooded eyes, letting her take her time, but she could see the tension in his jaw, could hear the need in his harsh breathing.

Hell, she could hear the need in *her* breathing, she could feel her need in the way her body vibrated around him, in how her hands gripped his shoulders tight.

"Nate," she whispered.

Then finally, she moved.

He gave her a moment – like, literally moments, to ride him slow, to roll her hips the way she knew they both liked, before his hands dug into her waist and his words were harsh and desperate. "Lou – please, can I ..."

She got to smile the devastating smile now as she nodded in response.

"Yes," she said. "Please."

And his desperation was *so* sexy as he flipped their positions. She wrapped her legs around his hips and held on as he slammed inside her again and again, murmuring praise and encouragement in her ear as he fucked her.

"You feel so good, baby, you're so fucking perfect ..."

Then, he pressed his thumb against her clit and she was coming all over again, her body breaking up into a thousand pieces as he groaned in her ear and spent himself inside her.

Afterwards, he rolled onto his back, dragging her along with him, so she lay curled against his chest.

Together, their breathing slowed and eventually, their skin cooled.

Then, without a word, Nate drew the sheets up and over their bodies.

And together they fell asleep.

CHAPTER SIXTEEN

NATE DIDN'T FALL ASLEEP.

Instead, he lay still as Lou relaxed against his chest, and listened as her breathing slowed into the steady cadence of slumber.

A few minutes after that, he reluctantly slid out from under her. She was so soft and warm and perfect against him, it seemed madness to extricate himself, but then, he was here for a reason.

And the reason had not been to spill his guts and then have mind-blowing sex with Lou. But he couldn't regret either.

It'd been true what he'd told Lou. He'd never questioned his decision to walk away from her until now. He'd hated himself for how he did it, but he'd always softened it with the supposedly knowledge it was for the best. A difficult decision, but the right one.

But now, tonight, he'd truly realised how wrong it had been.

How immature a decision it had been. How weak.

And how obvious it was now why he'd kept tabs on Lou for all these years. Quite simply, he'd missed her.

To be with her again like this, to be in her bedroom like this as she snuggled beneath the sheets in her sleep felt like a miracle. A miraculous opportunity for a do-over that he hadn't even realised he so desperately needed.

But – he wasn't stupid.

Lou was understandably wary around him. He didn't understand entirely why she'd slept with him again, other than she wanted too. He fully expected her to push him away again tomorrow morning, but he was going to work on that.

He just needed her to understand that—

Understand what?

Here, things got a bit fuzzy.

Nate pushed himself to his feet, and busied himself with the reason he wasn't sleeping – he needed to go check over the house. He pulled on his boxers, then padded on bare feet through the tiny house, checking each door, each window.

As he'd expected, everything was locked, and the house was a secure as a nineteenth century weatherboard cottage could be. Which was to say, should the Notechi really wish to get in, they wouldn't have any trouble at all. However – Nate would definitely hear them coming.

There was no unlocked door to slip through, or window to slide open.

Nate switched off the hallway and lounge room lights they'd left on and headed back to Lou's bedroom. She still slept, although she'd rolled onto her back, one arm flung across the side of the bed where he should be lying. Her hair was a banner across her pillow, much longer than when they'd been dating, and darker, appearing almost ebony against the crisp white of the linen in the moonlight.

So, should he hear the Notechi anywhere near Lou's property or breaking in, Nate's plan was to call Elite SWAT, and then do everything he could to keep her safe until they arrived.

Not exactly the perfect plan, but then he didn't have a CPP team, or surveillance, or even a firearm. Australian gun laws didn't allow him to just take his firearm home with him, and honestly, a tactical rifle wasn't something you could carry around in public, anyway. But, he did have a flick knife with him, in the backpack he'd just retrieved from Lou's living room, although it wouldn't be a hell of a lot of help against a bullet.

Still, it was something.

And he noticed Lou had a baseball bat propped against her dressing table, just as she had in her dodgy old share house bedroom. He remembered her shrugging when he'd commented on it back then: *Mum had a few shady boyfriends over the years. Figured if they ever tried to hurt Mum or me, it might come in handy.*

Fortunately, Lou's mum appeared to have dispatched all shady romantic interests before the baseball bat became necessary, but Nate had to commend Lou's thinking – both then, and now. It might come in handy, indeed.

But, most likely not.

Logically, it *still* made zero sense that anyone would come after Lou or him. It made much more sense that the shooter had deliberately missed Lou, and that the whole thing had been some stupid bikie gang idea of a show of strength. Probably aimed more at looking tough to the *other* OMCGs, rather than attempting to intimidate Elite SWAT. Which was a pointless pursuit, anyway.

Killing a police officer was about as stupid as it got, and there was no way the Notechi wanted the wrath of the WA Police Force descending upon them.

Surely.

Still. Nate still felt twitchy.

So, when he climbed back into bed with Lou, he didn't sleep.

He watched *her* sleep. And he kept his flick knife beneath his pillow.

NATE WOKE Lou just after five o'clock.

"What time is it?" she mumbled sleepily, rubbing at her eyes.

"Early," he confirmed. "Want to have a shower with me?"

She'd barely nodded in acquiescence when he'd scooped her up in his arms and carried her the short distance down the hall to her bathroom.

"Wha—?" she asked, when he placed her in front of the shower, then reached past her to flick on the taps.

She turned in a little circle as he watched her notice the fresh towels he'd retrieved from her linen cupboard, and that the small space was already warm from the heat lamp he'd turned on fifteen minutes ago.

"I've been awake for a while," he explained. In truth, he'd been going a bit mental just watching her sleep and counting the hours until he could reasonably wake her up. A night of admiring how beautiful she was in the moonlight – and pacing the house to check for marauding Notechis – had driven him crazy. His head was full of the need to protect this woman who slept so soundly beside him – and also the need to *have* her.

But he couldn't fully define what *have* her meant. Six hours of ruminating on what he was going to say to her this morning had achieved absolutely nothing. But he did know he'd need to move fast – sleepy Lou was less likely to kick him out of her house – and her life – as quickly as wide-awake Lou.

"Do you have a six o'clock start today?" she asked, as he gestured that the water was warm enough now and she could step into the shower.

"Nope," he said. He had today off actually, and tomorrow, in the lead up to night shift over the weekend.

Otherwise he never would've deliberately stayed

awake the way he had, knowing he'd have to potentially handle a firearm the next day. He had all day to sleep once Lou was safely at Elite SWAT HQ.

"So, you woke me up in the middle of the night because ...?"

Nate pulled the glass shower door shut behind himself. The shower stall was perfectly proportioned to the cottage – it was tiny – which perfectly suited Nate. They both stood beneath the bite of the water, shoulders bumping together.

"Because I wanted to have a shower with you," he said. "And celebrate not being murdered by the Notechi."

Lou smiled as she held her face up to the spray, her eyes shut as water streamed over her. "Isn't that my joke?" she teased, then added, "I suppose that *is* worth celebrating."

Nate pumped some soap out of the bottle in the shelf on the wall, and rubbed his hands together into a lather.

"Need some help getting clean?" he asked, and Lou's eyes popped open. He pantomimed soaping up an hourglass shape in demonstration.

"That's super cheesy, Nate," she said, laughing.

"Nope," he corrected. "It's genius. You get clean, I get to grope you. We all win."

She laughed again, but nodded amongst her giggles. "Sure," she said, even as she shook her head.

He started at her shoulders, the only part of her body he'd felt okay about caressing last night in her sleep without being a total sleaze. She sighed as he massaged the muscles there, her eyes sliding shut. "That feels good," she said, turning her back to him and lifting her now wet hair off her back and rearranging it to fall down her front and give him free access.

"I'm surprised I slept so well," she said. "Maybe I'm not so worried about the Notechi as I thought I was."

Nate's soapy hands slid from her shoulders to trace matching looping trails down either side of her spine. She was pliant beneath his touch, letting her body shift naturally under the pressure of his hands.

"Or maybe you just felt safe with me here," Nate said, and immediately Lou went still.

"Maybe," she said stiffly. "Or maybe I knew, deep down, E-SWAT were correct, and there is no threat."

To be honest, Nate had come to this conclusion himself at about three in the morning. The longer he sat in the dark waiting for a threat that seemed increasingly less likely to arrive, the more it seemed nuts to disregard the advice of the organisation Nate literally trusted with his life each day.

"Or maybe you just felt safe with me here," he repeated, knowing he was being stubborn, but suddenly needing Lou to acknowledge she'd felt protected. That she'd *needed* him here, in the same way he'd needed to protect her.

She turned around, and his hands fell back to his sides. "No," she said firmly. "I don't think that's the case at all."

"Really?" he said, and barked out a false laugh. "You would've slept just as soundly if you'd been alone last night?"

Her gaze narrowed. "Yes," she said. "I didn't need you here at all. If you remember, I didn't *want* you here at all."

Just like that, it was no longer clear if they were talking about fear, or the Notechi at all.

"I don't believe you," Nate said.

Lou shrugged. "Believe what you want."

"Really?" Nate said, stepping closer, knowing he was being a bastard by crowding her against the white wall tiles, but needing her to tell the truth.

He didn't touch her, but he was close enough to see the drops of water snagged on her eyelashes. "How about I believe you were relieved when I turned up on your doorstep last night. That I believe you were fucking scared but too stubborn to tell me, and too proud to admit it to Elite SWAT."

Lou shook her head, and she lifted her chin to hold his gaze. "No," she said.

Nate's gaze traced Lou's face – her expressive blue eyes, her strong nose, her stubborn jaw she'd lifted in defiance.

"How about I believe you're strong and brave," he said, his voice low and husky now. He watched as Lou's mouth dropped open in surprise. "That I believe I've never seen anyone as amazing as you were on that train yesterday. The way you stood up to Carey. The way you wouldn't cower when he could've shot you. The way you considered everyone else's safety before your own. You're even doing it right now – it's why you're not staying with your mum, or a friend, even though being alone last night fucking terrified you."

"Nate—"

"Lou, it doesn't make you less strong or less brave to want me here with you."

Her eyes flashed with annoyance. "That's ridiculous," she said. "Of course it does. Wanting you here is *not good,* Nate. It doesn't make me strong. It makes me feel useless, helpless. *Vulnerable.* I don't like it. I *hate it.*"

Her gaze was travelling all over his naked body, darting everywhere, settling nowhere. She'd curled her fingers into fists she kept at her side.

Yet, she didn't move away. Sure, he was standing close to her, but she had space to step around him. She was far from trapped. Yet she stayed. Close. With Nate.

He stepped even closer, the water hard against his back and lowered his head so he spoke into her ear.

"Wanting me here is bad, Lou?" he clarified. "Or just simply wanting me?"

She closed her eyes and rested the back of her head against the tiled wall. "You are so damn *smug,* Nate. So sure of yourself."

He arranged his lips into something like a smile. "I know you want me, Lou."

Lou snorted, and kept her attention on the ceiling.

"But I don't want you to hate wanting me. I don't

want that at all," he said. "Last night, and the night before – you wanted me against your better judgement. At the hotel it was a once-off. You told me that. Last night, you told yourself it was definitely the last time, right?"

She looked at him directly now. "It can't happen again."

He looked her up and down. Slowly, and deliberately. "Yet here you are, naked, with me."

"You caught me at a weak moment," she protested but with the ghost of a smile.

And her gaze had wandered now too, drifting from his face, to his chest, to his belly, then lower.

"Nate!" she said, as if she was surprised.

He laughed. "As I said, Lou, here you are, naked, with me. Seems a pretty obvious reaction, don't you think?"

She leaned back against the tiles again, once again staring at the ceiling, biting at her lip and taking deep breaths as if she was trying to focus. Remind herself why this was a bad idea.

But honestly, Nate couldn't work out right now how leaning forward to kiss the side of her neck was anything but the *best* idea. So, he did it.

He kissed her soft, damp skin, just below her jaw. And beneath his lips, he felt her pulse accelerate.

"Nate," she said, "how do you do this? I was literally just telling you – telling me, I don't know – that this can't happen again. That I don't *want* it to happen again. That I hate how wanting you makes me feel."

"Do you want me to stop?" he asked against her skin. "You know I will if you want me to."

She nodded.

Immediately he lifted his head and stepped away, disappointment hollow and heavy in his gut.

"I'm sorry Lou—" he began. *He'd been so sure she—*

"No!" she said, pushing herself away from the wall and flush against him, her hands flying up to snag behind his neck. "I meant, I know you'll stop if I want. Of course, I know that, Nate, but right now I don't want you to. No matter how much I hate it."

He still didn't like that, he didn't want hate having anything to do with what they had together.

But she was naked and pressed against him, and now she was tugging him down to her lips – and suddenly it all just felt like semantics. Hey, *wanting* was good. *This* was fucking good.

Her mouth was desperate beneath his, her kisses immediately deep and intense. She clung to him, pressed all the way down his body, his hardness pressed against her belly, the water still at his back.

He realised, very belatedly, that he was hogging all the water, and had been for some time. So, as he kissed her, he turned them both until it was Lou beneath the warmth of the water. Then, after he shaped the curve of her shoulders, waist and butt, he gripped her hips, breaking their kiss temporarily.

"Turn around," he murmured, and she did.

She pressed her back against him so the jets of water sprayed her chest and arms, and Nate's hands followed the journey of the water, cupping her breasts and sliding down her belly, slowly, slowly, until his fingers slid between her legs. She closed her eyes and rolled her head back against his shoulder, and he couldn't think of anything much more perfect than this. Than *Lou* – so perfect, so sexy, so trusting.

He explored her, loving how the water flowed in rivulets between her folds as he caressed her, before settling his fingers at her clit and circling the nub the way she liked. He loved how she sighed, and gasped and moaned as he touched her, as her body grew hotter and tighter, and as her hips began to shift against his touch, urging him on, wanting more.

"What do you want?" he asked, as he kissed his way along the curve of her neck.

"*You*," she breathed. "Please."

"Can you be more specific?" he asked, as his fingers on one hand pinched her nipple, and the other between her legs moved faster, harder.

She pushed her butt against his cock in response but he was enjoying this too much. Enjoying witnessing Lou wanting him, and losing herself in that want. She was so fucking beautiful, so perfect.

"My fingers?" he prompted. She was clearly capable of only nodding her head urgently at this stage, because the moment his pushed two fingers inside her heat, she was gone – her orgasm gripping his fingers as her hips undulated, her sighs and sounds of release rising louder than the beat of the water.

He wrapped his arm tight around her waist, anchoring her to him as the aftershocks faded, until eventually she lay still against him.

She looked up, and met his gaze.

Her hair was slicked back from her face, and her eyes were wide and clear, her lips a deep pink. She looked sated. Beautiful. But also, unsure.

Before she could say whatever she intended to say, he kissed her.

But this was a different kiss.

She was naked in his arms, but this wasn't about sex or his need for her that was absolutely raw and primal. This kiss was about the vulnerability she'd spoken of before that she hated. That supposedly made her feel weak, and useless.

But the vulnerability Nate was feeling now had nothing to do with the Notechi – which he was pretty sure Lou hadn't been talking about either. This was a vulnerability he felt deep down inside himself. Beneath all the layers of his identity – of being elite at what he did with a single-minded focus. Of making his father proud. Of being the man he'd always felt he'd wanted to be. That he'd expected himself to be.

Underneath all that was the young man who'd lost himself in Lou and – he realised now – had remained lost.

For all these years he thought he'd walked away from

the relationship that threatened his future, but he hadn't done that at all.

He'd walked away from the relationship that had exposed him in a way he couldn't handle. That had felt too big, too intense, too impossible to fit into the life he'd planned.

He'd been such a fucking idiot.

Because it was only now with Lou that he fully understood what he'd thrown away.

Suddenly, he knew exactly what he wanted to say to her, after the words had eluded him all night long.

He broke their kiss, but kept his mouth close to hers, so as he spoke, his lips brushed against hers.

"I *hate* that you hate wanting me, Lou," he said. He paused. Swallowed. "I want you to *love* wanting me."

She pulled back, putting too much space between them. "Love?" she said, with confusion in her gaze.

"Love," he repeated.

And then the water that still flowed over them turned cold.

CHAPTER SEVENTEEN

Lou rushed out of the shower — away from the frigid water, and also away from Nate.

She kept her back to him as she wrapped herself in a towel, but she could see Nate behind her in the mirror as he dried himself off and draped his charcoal coloured towel around his hips.

He met her gaze in the reflection. "Lou ..." he began.

But she shook her head, and darted past him before heading back to her room.

His footsteps were noisy behind her on the cottage's imperfect floorboards.

"You need to go," she said, as she yanked open the drawers of her dresser, randomly searching for underwear that she tugged on in jerky movements. With her bra straps halfway up her arms, Nate touched her elbow, and she sprang away as if burnt.

"*Don't*," she said. Then she had to make herself look

at him. He was still in his towel, still practically naked. The sun was yet to rise, so only a bedside lamp lit the room, but it was still enough light to make his skin glow golden. For every line and shadow of his body to be beautiful. "You *really* need to go. Now."

His gaze was hard and stubborn. "No," he said. "Not until you tell me why you're so upset."

Her bra on, she turned her back to him as she headed for her wardrobe. "This isn't funny, Nate," she said tightly.

"How could I possibly think it is?" he asked, and he sounded so genuinely surprised she turned on her heel.

"*Love*," she said. "Really? That's the word you chose?" She shook her head.

"What's wrong with love?" he asked.

"I don't know," she said. "Maybe I'm a bit sensitive because good things didn't really happen for me last time that word was thrown around between us. Okay?" She swallowed. Hell *yes,* she was sensitive about it. Hearing Nate say that word – even in the context of sex – was *not okay*. Because it had made her heart leap in a way that was completely unacceptable. "You were right when you said I'd told myself last night couldn't happen again. I had. And I'm telling myself again now. I'm telling *you* now. It's not going to happen again. Ever. So, you really, really need to go."

Lou closed her eyes, suddenly exhausted.

She couldn't believe she'd ended up here again: in a

place where Nate could hurt her. Because he could, so easily.

Last night, and in the shower, it was all too easy to imagine more nights, more showers, more intimacy, more *Nate*. In her house, in her life.

In her heart.

But then he'd gone and mentioned *love*, and the futility of her silly day dreams had been laid bare.

"I didn't just throw the word around, Lou," Nate said. He'd stepped up close to her. Not crowding her, not at all, as she reached back inside her wardrobe, and tugged on the nearest shirt in reach.

But as always, because he was close, he was *all* she was aware of.

"I *chose* that word," he continued. "Deliberately. After spending all night trying to figure out what I was going to say to you this morning."

This made her pause. She stood there in her shirt and knickers, staring at this tall, broad, naked man in her bedroom who was just so confusing.

"All night?" she asked.

He nodded. "I haven't slept," he said, "because – you know – potential murderous bikies in the vicinity, so I had a lot of time to think. To watch you sleep, and think about the past two days, as well as the past twelve years."

She shrugged, all nonchalant. "So, you want me to love having sex with you," she said. "Too easy. You win, I do. But it doesn't mean we're doing it again."

"*No,*" he said. "It wasn't about sex, Lou. It was about

wanting *you*. I want *you* in my life again. I want what we've had these past two days, and I want what we had twelve years ago – there's been no one else like you. I've never felt this way about anybody but you—"

"Haven't we covered this?" she interrupted, turning her back to him again and unclipping a skirt from its hanger. She didn't like how good Nate's words sounded to her, she didn't like it at all. "Remember? You were obsessed with me. We clearly have a really strong physical attraction, but surely, you're the last person to see that for more than it is."

She unzipped the skirt and stepped into it, then tugged it up over her hips. She had absolutely no idea if it matched the shirt she was wearing, but she wasn't capable of working that out right now.

"That would be true," Nate said, "if I didn't love you all those years ago. If I walked away because you loved me and I didn't feel the same way."

She zipped the skirt up violently, then met his gaze with a hard, narrow glare. "That is exactly what happened, Nate." She put her hands on her hips. "Please," she said, and she was horrified that her throat was tight and her eyes had begun to sting with unshed tears. *Why was she letting him do this to her again?* "Go."

He walked away, and her stomach sank which made no sense, right? Because she *wanted* him to do that. She *wanted* him to go.

In silence, he went to where his clothes were neatly piled up on the top of her dresser. She watched him drop his towel without hesitation, then pull on his boxer shorts, jeans, and T-shirt.

This was it. He was leaving. It was over. Again.

But he left his wallet, his phone and keys on the dresser as he walked back to her.

She hadn't moved – she'd barely breathed – since he'd walked away from her.

"I couldn't say this wearing just a towel, Lou," he began. His gaze was intense, like he was trying to look straight into her soul. "But that isn't what happened. It's what I told myself, but it wasn't what happened." He shut his eyes, squeezing them tight. "Fuck, Lou, I can still *see* you. Looking down at me and smiling, and telling me with such confidence that you loved me. I remember *everything* about that night. I remember you had a mozzie bite near your elbow. That you had pale yellow sheets on your bed. That you wore perfume that smelled like cake and how good your skin felt beneath my hands ..."

His eyes were open now, and Lou just couldn't look away as her body ignored every message her brain sent that she should. That she *had to*.

"I was obsessed with you, Lou, but I was in *love* with you. And I didn't realise that until today, but it's true. It's been true for twelve years, and baby – I think"—He took a deep breath—"I think I actually never stopped loving you. I think—"

"*Stop*," Lou said, reaching out and pressing a finger against his chest. "Just *stop* right now, Nathan Rivers.

You do *not* get to come back into my life after what you did and spout this crap, okay?"

Because it had to be crap. It couldn't be real.

She couldn't risk it being real, because then, what did that make her?

Vulnerable. And she *did not* want that.

"And it doesn't matter anyway. Haven't you listened to a thing I said? I didn't really love you. I was young and dumb, that's all. Dreaming of rainbows and a fantasy that doesn't exist. Whatever you think you feel, I know I don't feel it myself. I *know* it."

Could he tell she was telling this to herself as much as him?

Maybe. "Lou, come on ..."

But suddenly he went still. Silent.

Everything about him had become tense.

So tense, that she knew to speak in a whisper. "You heard something?"

He nodded, then soundlessly crept to his phone and rapidly typed a message before grabbing the wooden baseball bat she'd kept in her room for nearly twenty years, holding it easily in one hand. "Might be nothing," he said. "But I think it's something."

There was another sound now. Louder. More determined.

At her front door.

Like someone was trying to jimmy open her front door.

An image of displaced plant pots and soil flashed

across her brain, and fear started to grasp at her gut. To trail ticklish fingers down her spine.

"We stay here," Nate said, grasping her hand and leading her to the furthest point in her room from the door. He reached under his pillow on the unmade bed and handed her something.

A knife.

"Use this if you need to," he said. "Don't hesitate." He held her gaze.

"I won't," she said, and she goddamn hoped that was true.

Surely, she couldn't fuck up yet again? Not with her and Nate's lives on the line?

"Hide," Nate whispered urgently. "He can't see you when he walks in."

Whoever was at the door wasn't caring about silence now, and there was a crack as wood began to splinter.

She had a ridiculous, redundant moment of concern for the stained-glass door she loved before refocusing on concern for *her own life* and Nate's. She flicked the knife in her hand open and watched as Nate walked with determined steps to her open bedroom door before she dropped to a crouch beside her bed.

From here, she could see Nate reflected in the mirror hanging on the open door of her wardrobe.

He stood there – tucked against the wall beside the door architrave, the bat already held up and ready.

Old metal hinges creaked as the front door finally swung open. Footsteps moved heavy and swift down her hallway, the journey both terrifyingly short and mind-numbing long as fear and anticipation warred. She never wanted the stranger in her house to get here. She also wanted him here right now so this would end.

So Nate could end this.

It was the gun she saw first.

The man – and it was a man – held it in front of him with both hands, like some sort of bad TV police detective or something. But regardless, for a split second, that gun was all she saw reflected in the mirror in her bedroom doorway.

Then Nate moved.

Whoomp.

That was the sound the bat made as it flew through the air and hit flesh.

Thwack.

Was the sound it made when it hit bone.

And it hit bone. A lot of bones.

Once, twice, as the stranger in the hall fell to the ground, screaming as he clutched at his broken arm and attempted to scuttle in the direction of the fallen gun. A third time, *thwack*. To the side of his head.

And that was that. No more screams.

The house was silent.

Lou stood beside Nate, staring down at the intruder who was all dressed in black.

He was unconscious, his arm at all the wrong angles. Nate moved around her room and reappeared beside her with handcuffs he'd retrieved from his backpack. He swiftly cuffed the man's good arm to the broken one.

The stranger didn't move. Was he dead?

She considered checking for his pulse, but the idea of touching him revolted her. Even in the dark, the man was clearly a facsimile of Carey, all muscle and aggressive tattoos.

Nate retrieved the gun, and held it ready against his thigh. "I'm going to check he was alone," he said. "You stay here. E-SWAT shouldn't be long."

Lou barely had time to nod before he was moving, and she watched as he slipped in and out of her second bedroom before moving on to her lounge. A moment later, he was out the front door, leaving Lou half-dressed – her shirt untucked and feet bare – beside the unconscious or dead bulk of what was presumably a Notechi.

But before she could step back into her room for shoes – or to otherwise get ready for E-SWAT's imminent arrival, she heard something.

And before she had the opportunity to even register what it could be, an unfamiliar voice was right behind her.

"Drop the knife."

Lou flew to face the voice, and a shadow was before her. A *female* shaped shadow. The woman stepped forward, into the light thrown from the bathroom.

She held a gun in her hands, pointed directly at Lou's chest.

"If you scream," she said calmly, "I'll shoot."

The woman's gaze darted beyond Lou to the body on the floor behind her. Only for a second, then back to Lou, but it gave Lou enough time to notice the sheen of tears on the woman's cheeks. *Tears?* She also wore all black like the man on the floor – a singlet, jeans, boots.

"Drop," she said. "The. Knife."

She shifted the firearm, as if taking aim.

Thoughts raced through Lou's head. *Where was Nate? Where was the E-SWAT team?*

Her ears strained to hear him, or to hear approaching sirens but she heard neither.

She gripped the knife hard, trying to work out what to do.

"I've used this before," the woman said, again so, so, calmly. "Don't think I don't intend to use it."

Those words were so *resigned*, so empty – so absolutely believable – that Lou dropped the knife. She only needed to stop this woman from shooting for seconds probably, minutes at the most – before backup would arrive.

"Kick it to me," the woman said. "And *to* me. Not past me or I shoot. Got it?"

Lou nodded and did exactly what she was told.

She just needed to keep this woman calm. She took a deep breath. Then another.

Where was Nate?

The woman pocketed the knife in her jeans, the gun barely moving from where it was aimed at Lou's heart.

"On your knees," the woman said. "Now."

Lou dropped to the floor, and immediately the woman was beside her, the muzzle of her gun shoved hard against her temple. Lou looked up at the woman. She had long hair, neatly scraped off her face into a pony-tail, and her face was a study of tension – her jaw hard, her mouth drawn into a tight line. She'd *definitely* been crying.

Then she dropped to her own knees.

"Now let's wait for your boyfriend," the woman said softly.

"He's here." Nate's voice came from the kitchen. "Police," he said firmly. "Drop your weapon."

At his voice, the woman slid quickly behind Lou, barricading herself behind Lou's body.

As she moved, the gun moved with her, shuffling through Lou's hair until it pushed hard at the base of her skull.

"I don't think so," she said. "How about *you* drop your weapon, or I put a bullet through your girlfriend's brain?"

The gun pushed ever harder against Lou's skull, and literally all she could focus on now was where the barrel touched her. Maybe she'd still been adjusting to the fear, then the relief of what had happened with the male intruder, but only now did fear *fully* reassert itself. And it properly did. The woman's calm determination. The tears. The gun.

Lou was fucking terrified.

"Nate ..." she began, but she honestly had no idea what she was trying to say.

"An Elite SWAT team will be here any second," he said. "You're going to get caught. But if you stop this now—"

The woman laughed. "Drop your gun, SWAT-man," she repeated. "Drop it *now*."

It was impossible for Lou to see the woman's finger tighten on the trigger, but she sensed it. Every cell in her body sensed it.

"Please ..." she begged.

"Fine," Nate said tightly. His gaze kept flicking beyond the woman, as if he expected the E-SWAT team to storm the cottage at any moment.

The thing was, they might not have any moments to wait.

Nate held his hands and weapon in the air, then slowly placed the gun on the ground.

"Great," the woman said, and the bite of the gun's barrel was suddenly gone. "I have a new plan." She got to her feet. "You stay down there," she said, waving the gun at Lou. "And you, SWAT-man, you come over here. *Slowly*."

Nate did as he was told and also dropped to his knees only a metre or so from Lou.

The woman now stood between them in the hallway, training her gun first on Lou, then Nate.

"How about I shoot you first, so your girlfriend can

experience how it feels to watch someone murder their boyfriend?"

The words were so calm, so blasé, that it took a second for Lou to register their meaning.

But then, suddenly, the tears made sense. The not worrying about the police arriving made sense.

This woman didn't care if she got caught. She wanted revenge.

She shook her head. "Do you even know why we're here?" she asked neither of them in particular. "It's so fucking stupid. Shaun is – *was* – Brent's brother. You know the guy you killed? I *told* him not to do this. I told him to let it go, but here we are. And he's fucked up, and now *everything's* fucked up. The Notechi are going to be fucking *pissed*, and what am I going to do now?"

The tears had started again, trickling unheeded down her cheeks.

She'd been waving the gun about, but now she steadied it again and aimed it at Nate.

"Why did you have to do it? I mean, I get it, but still ..."

The calm veneer had cracked and fallen away completely. There was nothing blasé about her now.

Yet, her aim was steady.

Despite the tears, she was determined.

But the thing was, Lou had been watching Nate. Not directly, not obviously. But she'd been watching him.

Watching him as the woman rambled and delayed, and her attention lost its laser focus.

So, when out of nowhere, Nate smacked the gun out of the woman's hands, Lou was ready for it. And she was ready to grab the gun as it skittered along the jarrah floorboards, and the instant her hands gripped it, she was on her feet.

"Don't move!" she yelled.

But the woman did move, damnit, and suddenly that flick knife was in her hands.

She held it out in front of her body as she glared at Nate – totally ignoring Lou.

"See?" she said, "Everything is so fucked up. So very fucked up."

She shook her head, and stepped closer to Nate.

"Drop the knife," Lou said – loud and clear. Without hesitation. "Drop the knife, *now*."

But the woman wasn't going to drop it. She arced it in the air – not close enough to touch Nate. But close enough.

Lou didn't have to look at him to know he was working out how to disarm the woman.

But she also knew exactly how lethal that knife was.

"Drop the knife," Lou repeated. "Or I'll shoot."

This got the woman's attention. She swung her attention – and the knife – to face Lou.

"Really?" she asked. "You'd really shoot me? Right here, right now? Just because I won't drop this knife?"

Would she?

Lou studied the woman she was aiming the Glock at:

aimed exactly as she'd been trained, at her chest, the largest target on the body.

Lou tightened her finger on the trigger, just a little. Testing it, testing herself.

Her gaze flicked to Nate, who'd crept closer to the woman, to her side and just behind her.

Would she?

Lou nodded. And she knew, absolutely, that it was true.

She would shoot, she *could* shoot, if lethal force was required.

If she'd learnt anything from the past two days, it was that life could change in an instant.

She'd always known the responsibility she carried through being permitted to hold a firearm. For being permitted to use it – should the situation justify lethal force.

She'd delayed and delayed as a violent husband had threatened to kill her – because she'd held the responsibility of his daughters witnessing their father's death in her trigger finger. Yes, she'd delayed too long, and yes, she'd made a mistake – but she understood why she'd done it now.

It wasn't about being gutless, or being a failure.

And she'd paused – just for a *moment* – she realised now before she would've shot Carey on that train.

And she would've shot him. Her responsibility to protect the innocent victim – Fiona – would've made the decision easy. It was timing only, that meant it was the E-SWAT operator behind her that took the shot.

And all that responsibility was good. *Important*. Essential.

But she'd lost track of her other responsibility – her responsibility to *herself*.

To protect herself.

"You would do it, wouldn't you?" the woman said finally. Almost hopefully. Her gaze absolutely told Lou she believed her. Felt it deep inside her the way that Lou did too.

Lou held the woman's gaze. Strong, steady, determined. "But I won't have to," Lou said – just as Nate grabbed the woman's wrist and arm with both his hands, and threw her bodily across the narrow hallway, slamming the hand that held the knife hard against the wall.

The second slam dislodged the knife, and Lou grabbed it the moment it touched the floor – just as she registered the sound of rapidly approaching police sirens.

Nate held the woman's wrists tight behind her back, speaking as he met Lou's gaze over the woman's bowed dark head.

"You are under arrest...."

Lou didn't hear a word of the rest of what he said to the woman, but she certainly felt his gaze.

In it, she saw and felt *everything* that had happened between them – not just in the past few days, but *ever*, to right back at the beginning when she first saw Nate at the academy, at the gun range.

She felt the way it had started: the lust, the *obsession*, the connection. And she felt how it had ended: the betrayal. The abandonment. The rejection.

It seemed logical to take what she'd just learned – that she couldn't ever forget again to protect herself – as the reason why she should walk away from Nate.

Although it wouldn't be easy, of course.

It would be hard. Unbelievably hard. Impossibly hard.

Because, maybe like Nate said, she'd never stopped loving him.

An army of booted footsteps announced the arrival of the E-SWAT team – and then lights came on and people were everywhere, and Lou had no idea where Nate was.

But she knew, utterly and completely, that he would come find her.

He wasn't going to disappear from her life again, not unless she wanted him to.

But was that what she wanted?

CHAPTER EIGHTEEN

Nate raised his AR-15 and fired.

Once. Twice. Three times.

He lowered his arm as the body-shaped target continued its journey towards him, and he noted with some satisfaction the perfect arrangement of bullet holes upon the target's "heart".

He was the only operator at the indoor range today, and it was dim and silent now the shooting had stopped. His shift had finished an hour ago, but he couldn't quite motivate himself to go home.

He'd been like this each day since the incident at Lou's – feeling like he had too much energy, like he needed to keep his body busy. It had been just over a week, and he'd managed to get himself through his days off, and then night shift, then back to day shift starting again today by just absorbing himself in work and physical activity.

And trying not to think too much about Lou.

Ha.

Yeah, that wasn't going super well.

The last time he'd seen her was when they'd been interviewed back at Elite SWAT HQ, and he'd still been wearing jeans splattered with the Notechi intruder's blood. Lou had been strong and steady, and when it came to him, almost silent.

The guy he'd killed – and he had killed him, not that he could muster any regret – *was* a Notechi. But he hadn't been after Lou on Notechi orders. He'd been on his own personal crusade, seeking vengeance for his brother's death. So, the intel that E-SWAT had received was correct – they *had* been safe from the Notechi.

Just not from Carey's violent, vengeful brother.

The woman – his girlfriend – had been surprisingly helpful, and was continuing to assist Elite SWAT and Organised Crime in their enquiries. He'd heard whispers that she might take a deal in exchange for more intel, and so her involvement had been suppressed from the media.

So – it was over. The saga that had begun on a train and ended in Lou's hallway was done. He and Lou were safe. They could move on with their lives without looking over their shoulders.

Except Nate wasn't doing a real great job at moving on with his life.

His life, he realised now, was pretty fucking empty without Lou in it.

Twelve fucking years of emptiness. Yeah, twelve

years of a fulfilling career – sure. But what else did he have?

Not a hell of a lot.

What was super stupid, was now he knew *exactly* how deluded he'd been twelve years ago. Because in a week where he couldn't really get any *more* consumed by Lou, he'd lead two separate, complicated, successful jobs. A warrant out in the wheatbelt, and another just north of Perth. He'd been focused, skilled, clean and determined, as had his team.

Turns out he could separate work from love. And it *was* love.

He wondered now if his distraction all those years ago came from his struggles to comprehend what he was really feeling, rather than the relationship with Lou itself. Or maybe – and probably more likely – he'd simply been twenty-two and pretty immature. Just dumb, actually.

He was a grown man now. He absolutely knew what he was feeling, and he absolutely knew what he wanted: Lou.

But Lou, it seemed pretty bloody obvious – didn't want him.

Outside the interview room last week, he'd touched her arm when she would've otherwise walked away.

"Can I come over tonight?" he'd asked. "Or can I take you somewhere? A drink? Dinner? Coffee?"

Fuck, he hadn't cared. He'd just wanted to see her. Wanted to talk to her.

But she'd straightened her shoulders and answered

without hesitation. "No thanks, Nate," she said. "I need some time."

That was it. No further explanation.

But absolutely the fact that during their last conversation he'd declared his love for her – and she'd denied feeling any love for him – had hung between them.

Yet, she'd effortlessly walked away.

And stayed away. For eight long days, and longer nights.

Nate reloaded his gun and reset the target, but just before he put his ear protection back on, her heard someone enter the range.

He turned, and Lou was there. In jeans and a T-shirt, her hair tied back in a pony-tail.

"You here for some extra practise?" he asked.

He knew she'd started her firearm refresher training. Of course, he knew – he'd asked. He'd had to know something, *anything* about what she was doing.

"No," she said. "I never had an issue with my technique. I've always been a good shot. I still am."

Nate nodded. *So why was she here?*

She answered his unspoken question. "Can we talk?"

Of course, they could. He put his firearm on safe and took off his sling.

Then, he stood before her, in the viewing area adjacent to the range.

"I didn't hesitate that first night because I had an issue with firing a gun, Nate. I hesitated because I had an issue with my decision making."

She was standing just out of reach, and while her words sounded natural, her posture was subtly tense – he could see it in how she held her shoulders, and how her fingers played with the edge of her T-shirt. She was nervous. So was he.

"The training I'm doing now to get me back on full duties is good, of course. But it isn't really necessary. I've worked it out myself, and I know – I absolutely know – that I won't put myself in a position where I put myself, or anyone else, at risk through my own hesitation to use my weapon."

"I know that too," Nate said. "I knew you had me covered in that hallway."

He'd never had a shred of doubt that she would protect him.

"Thank you," she said and looked pleased. "I'm glad you knew that."

It took everything he had not to reach for her – not to tell her *of course he knew that.* That he had absolute faith in her.

"It's easy, you know," Lou continued, "to get caught up in a moment. To think about so many potential consequences that you lose focus on what's really important. I need to do my job well, and I need to make measured decisions – but I also need to protect myself." She paused. "I think you can work out where this is going."

"You need to protect yourself from me."

She nodded, and Nate took a deep, slow breath as his stomach plummeted.

"Yes," she said softly. "That's what I've been doing this past week. Protecting myself – my *heart* – from you."

Those words settled around them. This past week – this endless, lonely week without Lou. And yet ...

"And yet, you're here," he said.

"I'm here," she said, but something in her gaze had him far from rejoicing. "Because I wanted to ask you something."

"Anything," he said. He'd answer anything, give her anything.

"On the train, you were distracted by me, weren't you? It's how Carey got up, it's how he had the chance to grab Fiona."

"Yes," he said.

"But that's why you left before, isn't it? Because having me in your life threatened your career. What's changed now?"

Oh, this was easy. "Everything's changed," he said. "I'm not afraid of love any more, Lou. I'm not afraid of how I feel about you and what it means to me to have you in my life. And while I hope to god we're not held hostage together *ever* again – because I'm telling you right now, I'll never be fucking calm and rational and at my best when the woman I love has a gun pointed at her – loving you threatens nothing, except ..." He swallowed. "My heart."

And *how* it threatened it. It felt raw and exposed. All of him felt raw and exposed as he stood here in front of Lou, waiting.

Waiting for her to make a decision, when she'd just told him she'd spent a week reflecting on making *good* decisions. Good decisions that protected her from harm.

And he'd hurt her, bad.

"The thing about protecting myself, Nate," Lou said. "Is working out why I'm doing it. Obviously, most importantly, I need to protect myself for *me*. I need to put myself first, as hard as it might be at times. I *have* to do that. I *have* to."

He didn't stop staring into her eyes, no matter how much it hurt. Into her deep blue-green gaze that was *so* full of emotion. Emotion he couldn't define – not yet.

"And I *will* do that, Nate. Of course, I will. But also, when I protect myself at work, I'm doing it for me and for those I love. My mum, my family, my friends. I don't want to not be there for them. I need to protect myself for them. And –" She stepped closer. Close enough to touch. "Last week in the hallway, I realised I wanted to protect myself for *you*. So, amidst my need to protect myself *from* you and how vulnerable you make me feel, I know that I need you in my life, Nate. You're the man I want to come home to after each shift. You're the man I ..."

Her gaze dipped now, landing somewhere near their toes.

She took a deep breath. Straightened her shoulders.

She met his gaze again. "You're the man I love, Nate," she said. "I love you. And you were right – I always have. I never stopped, no matter how badly I wanted to."

He *had* to touch her now. And he did, reaching out to lace his fingers with hers.

She held on tight.

"I won't ever hurt you again, Lou," he said and meant that with every cell in his body.

She laughed, which kind of dented the sentiment.

"You don't know that," she said, her eyes sparkling. "And neither do I. I could hurt you, too, you know – that's just part of the deal, right?" She stepped closer again, so their chests almost brushed together. "But you know what's crazy? That doesn't matter any more. I *know* you love me and that I love you, and that love is complicated and risky and vulnerable. But I *want* to feel that with you. I want *everything* with you, Nate."

He leaned down, and brushed his lips against hers, holding her hands tight so he didn't wrap his arms around her to pull her hard against his body.

"I love you so much, Lou," he said. "I want everything with you, too. The obsession and the fantasy of twelve years ago, and the reality and the future of now." He grinned. "Actually, I'm still totally obsessed with you, just so you know."

She untangled her fingers to slide her hands up to his shoulders, and she pushed herself up on her tiptoes as she spoke against his lips. "Oh, I'm still *totally* obsessed with you, Nate. I don't think that's ever going to change."

"It won't," he said with utter confidence as he dragged her into his arms. "This is us, Lou. Together, obsessed, in love."

She kissed him hard and long, and he kissed her right back.

"Sounds good to me," she said, on a ragged breath. "Um – can you take me home, or somewhere – close – please? Now?"

His grinned a wicked grin. "We met at a gun range, Lou. Might as well start the next stage of our lives together at one, too."

They both laughed as he pressed her up against the nearest wall, until their mouths were busy with other delicious, naughty things.

And it was good. So, so, very good.

ACKNOWLEDGMENTS

For the Fight is my tenth book, but my first romantic suspense, and my first self-published novel. Writing and publishing Lou and Nate's story has been a steep learning curve, and wouldn't have been possible without a lot of help and support.

Thank you to Linley Maroney, for leaping together with me on this new self-publishing adventure. It is so much better sharing this with you!

Thank you also to Rachael Johns for giving me the most public of deadlines (The West Coast Fiction Festival), and for all our Voxer conversations.

I'd also like to thank my editor, LaVerne Clark, who squeezed my edits in so I could meet Rach's public deadline! I really appreciate it.

And lastly, thank you to my incredibly supportive family, who really listen when I ramble on about my books and support me every step of the way. Whether with brainstorming, babysitting, a Mac I can format books with (thanks Annie!), or simply asking me how the book is going - I couldn't do this without you.

ABOUT THE AUTHOR

WWW.LEAH-ASHTON.COM

RITA® Award-winning author Leah Ashton writes fast-paced, sexy romantic suspense and smart, modern contemporary romance. All her books feature strong heroines, deliciously heroic heroes and swoon worthy happily ever afters.

Leah lives in Perth, Western Australia with her gorgeous husband, two amazing daughters and the best intentions to meal plan and have an effortlessly tidy home. When she's not writing, Leah loves all day breakfast, rambling conversations and laughing until she cries. She really hates cucumber. And scary movies.

facebook.com/leahashtonauthor

bookbub.com/authors/leah-ashton

ALSO BY LEAH ASHTON

Elite SWAT Series

Books can be read in any order

For the Fight

Out Run the Night

Danger in Trust

Explosive (prequel novella)

Contemporary Romance

Note: Unlike my romantic suspense novels, all my contemporary romances are "closed door" love scenes, except for Nine Month Countdown.

Secrets & Speed Dating

A Girl Less Ordinary

Why Resist a Rebel?

Beware of the Boss

Nine Month Countdown (Molyneux Sisters #1)

The Billionaire from her Past (Molyneux Sisters #2)

Behind the Billionaire's Guarded Heart (Molyneux Sisters #3)

The Prince's Fake Fiancee (Vela Ada #1)

His Pregnant Christmas Princess (Vela Ada #2)

Mining for Love (trade anthology of the Molyneux Sisters)

Lightning Source UK Ltd.
Milton Keynes UK
UKHW041620210222
399003UK00004B/862

9 780648 440062